SHADOWS
ON MY SOUL

LEIGH JARRETT

Published by Steambath Press (self-published)
Editor: Alyson Pearce at Between the Lines

Paperback edition published June 2017
ISBN-13: 978-1927553374
ISBN-10: 1927553377

Dedication

I want to thank those that assisted me with my research, Jazzy, Sandy, and the last minute surprise, Annie, one of my beta readers, who, after reading the book, informed me she works with sexual assault victims. Whether it was documented facts, common myths, or sharing the stories of others. Every piece helped me create Justin. Thank you so much for your crucial input.

I'd also like to thank my beta readers, who as always, put up with my barrage of constant changes. And who, this time around, braved the difficult content of this book. I promise, my next book will be steering back toward Fantasy and Sci-Fi. The vampire wars are coming!

And most importantly, I'd like to thank my wife. The writing of this book took a toll on me, both emotionally and physically at times, which is why it took me three years to finish it. She continued to support me when I'm sure she felt like finding a vacation home away from me. Thank you, sweetness. I love you so much.

Foreword

A word about the format of this book. You will note there are large sections of this book written in italics. These italicized paragraphs represent the character, either Derek or Justin, thinking back, remembering, and/or reminiscing about conversations, events, and emotions they had in the past. This is important to keep in mind as you read this book.

Chapter One

Justin's glare shot across the truck, imploring Derek to *shut the fuck up*. Tears were cutting agonizing streaks down his cheeks.

Derek set his attention back on the road, adjusting his grip on the wheel. He glanced over in Justin's direction again. The man he loved was tucked up shivering against the cold glass of the passenger seat window, his breath creating an ebb and flow of opaque mist obscuring the blackness beyond, a mournful silence descending upon them.

If only he could reach out.

The lights from passing cars illuminated Justin's face, then plunged it into darkness, each glimpse of the familiar features mutilated into something unknown, defeated ...destroyed.

He'd never seen a man look so broken.

Damn it, Justin.

The evening had begun innocently enough.

Chapter Two

Lake Nootkum, nestled amongst the old-growth, evergreen forests of Harrop County, Washington, with its serene, smooth pebbled shores, shady fishing nooks, and deep throaty vibrations of ravens overhead, was awe-inspiring at any time of year, but in the spring, not long after the last vestiges of snow had disappeared, the crisp, pungent air, rich with the scent of cedar and pine and moist, mossy earth had a way of reminding one that as human beings we were connected in our origin. That the abundance and beauty of nature was still our home.

A connection that stirred Derek Lawrence's soul.

Derek loved being outdoors working up a sweat as he labored in the elements and toiled to provide the requirements for survival. It brought him a sense of inner peace. Each time he left the tranquility of this place to return to his daily life, Derek felt revived.

Right now though, he had something else on his mind.

A big, beautiful thing that could not be ignored.

His ax came down swift and precise, splitting the log perfectly down the middle. Years of practice had developed his wood-splitting skills to a science, leaving him free to use the strenuous activity for gains other than merely the provision of firewood.

Especially when one was camping within an active, woodland campground.

He straightened up, leaned the ax handle against his thigh, and rubbed the thick dark scruff along his jawline with his knuckles. He scanned his surroundings to see if anyone was watching his muscle-rippling display. He'd hoped his gorgeous neighbor in the next campsite over was still hovering around outside his tent, but he must've headed back toward the lake to do some more fishing.

Derek wiped his hands on the paint-spattered, threadbare jeans he'd reluctantly retired from the job sites of late, his fingers continually becoming tangled in the shaggy-edged holes.

With his target nowhere to be found, he decided to give up on his current quest, and turned back to his own campsite, helpless to contain a grin of satisfaction.

They had their long-standing group together this weekend as they did most weekends. Sam and his wife, Karen, and their one-year-old daughter, Brittany, the least fussy baby he'd ever laid eyes on, and his best friend and business partner, Justin Leary.

Derek observed the dynamics of the group.

Sam's cousin, Nick, had come along as well. He was only in town for a few days, so they'd invited him to join them. He seemed all right. Maybe a bit quiet, but then the rest of the group was so damn noisy Nick was likely struggling to establish his bearings before speaking up.

"Hey, Derek," Justin shouted, waving his arm over his head. "Any luck?"

"Nah," Derek replied as he headed toward their fire pit, arms laden with a stack of split firewood. "I think he's taken off for a while."

"Bummer," Justin said, then snorted beer out through his nose. He slapped his hand on his thigh while laughing and gasping for air, almost falling off the log he was sitting on.

"Oh, my god, *bum*mer, get it?" He coughed and cleared the spilled beer from his face with the back of his hand. "That was priceless."

Derek grinned. Justin Leary, with his boyish goofiness and shocks of blond hair sticking out in all manner of directions, every crease and laugh line deepening with jubilance, every gasping breath accentuated by his mischievous eyes, hadn't even noticed no one else was laughing.

His best friend was a lunatic. There was no other possible explanation. It was a characteristic of Justin's personality that he wouldn't want Justin to abandon. Not around him anyway.

And despite Justin's near-constant antics, *Lawrence & Leary Custom Homes & Renovation* wouldn't be the same without him. Justin was incredible to work with. His ideas and expertise had helped propel their company to the forefront of contractors in the area.

Unfortunately, Justin's lighthearted approach to life was likely the reason he hadn't had any luck with girlfriends over the years. The guy was such a goof women never took him seriously. And that bothered him. Derek wanted Justin to find happiness. To marry and start a family.

A life Justin often spoke of wanting.

Derek released a heavy sigh, turned away, and zipped up his vest against the cold after dumping the split wood atop the pile he'd been amassing fireside. The sun had begun its retreat behind the western tree line. The deep chill of an early April night would be descending upon them soon.

The sound of Justin discarding an empty beer bottle atop the brown glass menagerie accumulating at his feet had Derek glancing back over at him. His breath caught, and he looked away. He needed to focus on something else—anything else. Justin had opened another beer and set it to his lips. Lips that remained damp and moist with every sip he took.

Breathe.

Derek massaged the back of his neck with the palm of his hand as he stared into the fire. His relationship with Justin was never going to be anything more than friendship.

It just wasn't.

Nick shifted his weight on the log he was perched upon, and tucked his knees up as he clutched his beer in one hand. "What if he's not gay?"

"That's never stopped Derek before," Karen said as she adjusted Brittany in her lap. "You've been fucked by plenty of straight boys haven't you, sweetheart?"

Derek wrinkled his brow. "Not now, Karen." The color had drained from Nick's face, and his knees were bouncing up and down.

"I don't think Nick wants to hear about any of that," Sam said as he chucked a handful of twigs and bark remnants at the fire, disturbing the flames, then he glared into the embers.

Karen narrowed her eyes at Sam and rubbed her nose as she turned to face Nick. "I'm sorry, Nick. We've known Derek since high school." She ruffled her hair, loosening the messy bun at the nape of her neck. A dark tendril escaped, landing on her cheek. "I sometimes forget to keep things clean and *straight* when there's someone new around."

She pointed in Sam's direction. "Ask my husband."

Sam's only response was a low, grunting laugh.

Nick shook his head. "No, it's all right. You caught me off guard is all." He finished his beer and twisted the empty bottle into the dirt between his boots, grinding it in with more force than Derek thought necessary. It was time to change the subject.

"You want another," Derek asked as he flipped the cooler open. When Nick nodded, he opened two, handing him one.

"So, what's on the agenda for this evening?" Justin asked as he clapped his hands together. "I've worked out some new songs."

Derek glanced over at the guitar case resting against the log behind Justin. It was never far from his side. Not that Justin was great at playing it mind you. Justin's real talent as far as Derek was concerned, was his voice. A voice he'd become accustomed to hearing echoing throughout every job site they'd ever worked on over the past ten years as Justin rarely stopped singing.

Whether you wanted him to or not.

"Well," Sam replied. "I've been up to my ears in depositions this past week, so I thought we'd start by drinking to clear my head." He jabbed the fire with a stick, sending amber sparks into the air. "And then I thought we'd do some more drinking, to make sure I can't remember a thing about work."

Karen poked Sam in the ribs, making him gasp and clutch his side. "All right—all right. Only until I've expunged those ludicrously conflicting statements from my mind, I promise."

"Fine." Karen handed Brittany to Sam. "But someone needs to help me with the dishes first."

"I can help you." Derek set his beer down, reached for the plastic water container, and gave it a shake. It was predictably empty. Justin had likely drunk it all. The guy always seemed to be thirsty and hungry. He couldn't understand why more of it hadn't stuck to Justin's lean muscular frame, which was currently hovering over the campfire, poking away at the embers to encourage the new wood he'd tossed onto the blazing inferno to catch fire.

"That ought to do it for now," Justin exclaimed as he brushed some debris from the logs off his hands onto his jeans.

Derek rolled his shoulders in an attempt to relieve the tension. He knew from experience there was little he could do to stave off the inevitable *drunk Justin* weekend ahead of them. The blaze was stoked to burn for hours, which meant Justin was planning to drown himself in alcohol …again. An attempt to chase off whatever demons always seemed to be plaguing him.

Justin refused to talk about it, and Derek had stopped pushing for an answer to his best friend's pain years ago.

"Derek! Dishes."

"Right, sorry."

Derek smirked. He would have to head down to the tap near the lake to fill the water container. Perhaps sexy *camper-guy* would be down there somewhere. A few well-placed smiles and looks might change the course of his evening. Maybe his entire night if he was lucky and their neighbor had enough stamina to match his own. The guy had the muscular bulk to provide a challenge. It would take a fair amount of grappling before he'd relent and submit to him.

Plus, finding somewhere to sleep that involved a little extracurricular activity before bedtime suited him better than bunking with Justin. Not that he minded sharing a tent with him. He'd been doing it for years, but Justin tended to snore, mumbled in his sleep, and *always* ended up with his arm draped over Derek's body. Which more often than not, set Derek's cock off. And that was a line he was unwilling to cross. Regardless of his feelings for Justin, releasing a load in his sleeping bag next to him would definitely cross that line.

Derek pulled at his vest. The temptation to reach out during the night and stroke Justin's face, brush his fingers across Justin's sexy ginger stubble or kiss his lips—it had a way of twisting his guts up. He was better off in a different tent.

"We're out of water," Derek announced, followed by a wink in Karen's direction.

Karen's eyes narrowed. "Don't you dare. I'll send someone else to retrieve the water if you're going to bugger off."

Justin shot his second stream of beer out through his nose.

Sam turned on him, his jaw clenched.

"Grow up, Justin."

Justin snorted through a laugh.

"But she said *bugger* ..."

Nick exhaled through his nose, pulled himself to his feet, and trudged off down a small trail through the trees in the direction of a creek that fed the lake below.

"Nice," Sam said. "Scare my cousin off into the woods. Is it really so difficult to contain yourselves for one damn weekend?" He rose to his feet, juggling Brittany on his hip. "Karen, seriously. Nick did not need to hear about Derek's voracious, gay sexual habits."

Derek crossed his arms. Sam's comment about his relationships being *gay sexual habits* had stung. And *voracious*?

He wasn't that bad.

Okay, maybe he was.

"I apologized," Karen replied.

"Well, I'm sick of it." Sam's body tensed as he cut a circle through the air with his free arm. "The jokes, the innuendos, the ridiculous denial." He stabbed a finger at Justin. "Weekend after weekend. Year after year. It's the same damn thing between the two of you."

"Sam, it's not—," Justin said.

"It is." Sam redirected his attention onto Derek. "I am stunned you two manage to run a business together."

Derek reached out toward Sam. "Hey, look, let's—"

"No." Sam glared at each man in turn, then set his focus on Justin. "I wish you would just fuck Derek, or do whatever it takes, so the rest of us can have some peace."

There was a moment of shocked silence, amplifying the serene sounds of the forest, surrounding campers, and crackling fires.

Justin erupted to his feet.

"Fuck off, Sam!" He spat at the ground, his face reddening as he paced back and forth on a small area of gravel at the edge of the fire. "You know nothing about Derek and me."

He jabbed a finger in Sam's direction, punctuating his words. "Even if I was gay. Which I am not. I wouldn't be the least bit interested in Derek."

And there it was.

Derek looked down at his feet, scuffing the tiny bits of gray stone back and forth with his boots, willing his expression and the heartache and pain hovering there, to relinquish.

"You have no idea what you're talking about," Justin added.

"Really?" Sam countered as he swung Brittany to his other hip. "When I first met the two of you, I thought you were together. It took me by total surprise that you weren't."

"Okay, that's enough." Karen jammed a clenched fist to her

waist. "Is anyone planning on going after Nick? He might get lost out there."

Justin chucked his beer at the fire, sending a cluster of sparks up into the air, and stormed off toward the trail. "I'll go after him," he shouted over his shoulder. "I have my walkie-talkie. Let me know if he makes it back before I do."

As Justin disappeared into the underbrush, Derek sunk onto a log and stared up at Sam. "What the hell was that about? Why did you feel the need to bring all of that up again?"

"You don't see it, do you?" Sam replied while shaking his head at Derek.

"See what?" Derek furrowed his brow as he prepared to argue with Sam—again. In high school, Sam had tried to convince him that Justin had a severe crush on him. And curious as to whether or not Sam was on to something, he had approached Justin about it.

And Justin had almost fallen off the bleachers laughing.

The bleachers were damp, but that wasn't about to deter either one of them. Anything was better than heading back inside to face the latest request for them to report to the principal's office. Most likely for something Sam had done.

"This is bullshit," Justin repeated, combing a hand through his hair. "My mom is going to kill me if I get suspended again."

"Yeah," Derek replied. "At this rate, we're never going to graduate."

Justin grinned.

"Yup," he said. "We might have to kill him."

Derek shoved Justin, almost toppling him over, and then pulled at Justin's sleeve to right him, and took a deep breath.

The idea of Justin being interested in him was absurd. He'd told Sam that, but if Sam were right ...that would change everything. Everything he and Justin held to be true about their relationship. Just friends. They'd always been just friends.

"What's up?" Justin asked, eyeing the expression on Derek's face. "You look like you're about to throw up." He shifted down the bleacher seat a few inches to place some distance between him and Derek. "Don't tell me that flu has come back on you."

"Nah." Derek shook his head in an attempt to dismiss the possibility that Justin's feelings for him went beyond friendship. Sam hadn't been able to shut up about it, and some of the points Sam had made were valid. He glanced over at Justin and smiled. The guy was everything he was looking for in a boyfriend.

"What?" Justin said, wrinkling his brow. "You better spit it out, or I'll have to wrestle it out of you."

Derek snorted through a laugh. That would be poignant given the thoughts whirling around in his head.

He decided to spit it out. Get it over with.

"Sam was talking at me yesterday," Derek said, then grinned, knowing Justin would understand the distinction of being talked at.

"Yeah, and—?" Justin replied.

"He thinks," Derek began, then stopped. Approaching Justin about this was ridiculous. The fact he was asking at all ...except he needed to know.

"He thinks," Derek began again, "that you might ..." He stomped his feet on the bleacher in front of him. This was stupid. "Never mind," he said and wrapped his arms across his chest to stay warm. The forecast was calling for snow, and it looked as if the weather forecast might be correct for a change.

"Oh no, you don't," Justin said. "What might I?"

Derek rolled his shoulders. "Sam thinks you might have feelings for me." He peered over at Justin, awaiting his response.

"Like feelings, feelings?"

"Yeah, it's stupid," Derek replied, shaking his head as an extended silence permeated the frigid air, giving Derek a glimmering moment of hope that Justin might have feelings for him after all. That Sam had been right.

The snort and giggle gave away the direction of Justin's impending response. Then the full-on laughter started, almost propelling Justin off the edge of the bleachers.

Derek decided to laugh along with him, to hide the disappointment—and embarrassment. It had been ridiculous to hope for something as incredible as Justin's affection.

Derek stroked his hand along his thigh, dismissing a memory that already spent far too much time in the forefront of his mind. It paled in comparison to the absolute rejection Justin had leveled at him tonight.

"Forget it," Sam said. "Even if Justin is in love with you, I don't think he'll ever fess up to it. Not to you anyway."

"Wait," Derek said, returning to the conversation. "What do you mean, not to me? Has Justin said anything to you?"

He looked back and forth between Sam and Karen. "To either of you."

Sam shrugged in silence, but Karen spoke.

"He doesn't have to," she answered. "When he's hanging with us and knows you're off hooking up with some random guy …"

"His over the top, jocular repertoire can only cover up so much," Sam said, then kissed his daughter's forehead as he cradled her in his arms. "Seriously, buddy. It's brutal to watch."

Karen dried her hands off on a tea towel and set it to one side. "In all the time you've known him, surely you've noticed that Justin always seems to be battling something."

Derek scowled, setting his thumb at his temple, his fingers tracing a succession of circles on his brow. He stared up into the canopy of cedar boughs as if they might offer him some clarity.

"Derek?" Karen said, drawing his attention back.

"Yes," Derek replied. "I've noticed, okay."

"And?"

"Why do you think it has anything to do with me," Derek

replied. "I asked him about this in high school. I asked Justin if he was interested in me and he almost bust a gut laughing."

Sam snorted in amusement. "Jeez, Derek. I had no idea you'd asked him. You must've thrown him right off. He didn't even know you were gay. None of us did."

"I'm not entirely sure that's true," Derek replied.

Karen crossed her arms, watching Derek.

"So," she said, "you think Justin knew? He knew you were gay?"

"I don't know." Derek shrugged. "Maybe."

Karen reached for him, but he scowled and strode off toward his tent as he replayed portions of the past sixteen years in his mind. He searched for anything that might back up or unequivocally negate what Sam and Karen were saying, ignoring Karen's calls to come back.

Justin had been a constant presence in his life since they'd met the summer before starting their junior year at high school. They'd hit it off immediately and become inseparable, spending an incredible last three weeks of summer together. Their days filled with epic biking adventures, thigh-burning hikes, regular sugar overdoses, and midnight skinny-dips in the nearby lake.

Derek smiled. He'd completely corrupted Justin that summer. And for every summer after that when they weren't picking up odd jobs around local construction sites.

From his perspective, it had seemed a natural progression for them to enroll in a trade school together after graduating, but Justin *had* been reluctant. He hadn't warmed up to the idea of enrolling in construction courses straight out of high school.

Not right away at least.

Not until after a night of playing video games and watching movies together at Justin's parents' house. They'd passed out on the sofa in the den, and he'd awoken the following morning with Justin's arm draped over his body amidst a jumble of Xbox controllers and cables.

He hadn't been ready to get up, so he'd tossed the controllers onto the floor and tucked himself back against Justin's body. The sleeping arrangement wasn't that different from what usually happened when they were camping. Maybe a little closer than usual, but Justin hadn't seemed to mind. He'd only grumbled about not wanting to be pulled along if Derek fell onto the floor.

Of course, Derek hadn't slept much after that. The feel of Justin's chest pressed against his back—and his warm breath tickling the hairs on the nape of his neck had made him so hard he'd had to battle the urge to grind his ass back against Justin's body.

The next day, they'd gone online and registered for the first of many construction courses they'd take at the local trade school over the next few years.

Maybe Justin hadn't wanted to pursue a career in construction.

Maybe Justin had put his own aspirations on hold for him.

No, he wouldn't do that.

"How can you be so sure Justin's gay?" Derek asked as he made his way back to where Karen was tossing the dirty dishes into a small plastic tub. "Did he come out to either of you?"

"And that would make a difference, how?" Karen asked. "He's your goddamned best friend, Derek. The fact you're giving this any consideration at all speaks volumes. Whether he's *officially* gay or not is completely beside the point."

Derek swore beneath his breath as Karen waved a dismissive hand at him.

"Shh, here they come," she whispered.

Derek jammed his hands into his pockets. This situation was beyond awkward. Now he'd be measuring Justin's every word. Every decision. Every look. The uncertainty of Justin's feelings toward him was going to affect their business dealings. It was going to change everything.

As Justin and Nick approached, Derek was unable to take

his eyes off the familiar gait as it brought Justin back to the fire's side. Tracking the fluid motion of Justin's body, Derek couldn't turn away. The man did incredible things to his insides. He gripped his stomach in an attempt to still it when Justin looked over at him, his lips illuminated by the firelight as he smiled at him.

The accompanying wink almost brought Derek to his knees.

Karen was right. There was something.

And there had been for a long time.

Chapter Three

"Get this guy a beer, would you," Justin said to Derek as he passed by him. When Derek didn't respond, Justin turned back.

"You okay?" he asked, laying a hand on Derek's shoulder.

"Yeah." Derek nodded. "I'm fine."

"Good." Justin pounded Derek on the back. "And no more talk about stalking our campsite neighbor. Turns out Nick knows the guy. His name's Rocky. And from what little he told me about him ...you do *not* want to be fucking with that guy."

Derek studied the changing expression on Nick's face as Justin spoke. He couldn't be sure of the reason, but Rocky had done something to him that had scarred him. Lingering apprehension and a heavy dose of revulsion blackened his eyes.

"High school?" Derek guessed, and Nick nodded.

Derek set his hand on his hip, nodding, then looked away. That would be the end of the discussion. Sam's cousin didn't seem like the sharing type.

"Let me get you that beer," he said to Nick.

Nick looked to be mid-twenties. Almost ten years younger than the rest of them, but still a long stretch of time since high school. The pain of whatever Rocky had done to him was still fresh and might explain his shy nature. Or maybe his shyness had been the reason he had been picked on. It wasn't because of his size. Nick was a big guy. From what Sam had told them, he'd been a successful linebacker all the way through high school and the first few years of college.

Justin moved closer to Derek and tugged the edge of his jean's pocket to get his attention.

"Derek."

Don't. Please don't do that.

Derek hated when Justin did that. That simple tug always carried him to a place where he could practically feel Justin wrenching at his belt buckle, unlatching it.

Damn, Justin.

His legs threatened to turn to jelly.

"Do you mind if Nick shares our tent?" Justin asked, nudging Derek with his elbow. "He's worried about being on his own in the same campsite as that guy."

"What the hell did he do to him?" Derek whispered to Justin, wanting to keep Nick, who was back in front of the fire, from overhearing them. The distance was minimal, but he seemed to be ignoring them, busily rearranging the logs.

Justin shrugged his shoulders. "He won't tell me."

"Yeah, I figured," Derek replied.

"Guys, it's fine," Nick called from the far side of the fire. He jammed a stick into the base of a log, chipping away the petal-shaped bark rimmed in the white and orange of impending ash.

The log hissed and popped, then fell, crackling sparks into the air, obscuring him for a moment.

"I passed him on the way to the washrooms earlier," Nick continued. "I don't think he recognized me. I'm probably being paranoid."

Justin shoved Derek, knocking him backward.

"Derek—"

Derek shoved Justin back.

"Justin—"

Justin raised his eyebrows and tipped his head in Nick's direction.

Derek rolled his eyes. He'd wanted a few moments alone with Justin. Time to talk things through. Maybe find out where they stood with each other.

He closed his eyes, disappointed. It would have to wait until tomorrow. He'd suggest a hike to Justin in the morning. They were bound to find somewhere they could talk uninterrupted.

As for tonight, Nick's last minute decision to join them meant he'd had little chance of securing a site next to theirs. Either he or Justin would have to make the trek up to the empty group camping area further into the trees where Nick had set up his tent.

There wasn't enough room in their tent for three men.

"Sure." Derek cocked his head toward their tent. "But we're not all going to fit in there. The two of us barely have room enough to move around without ending up all over each other."

There was a moment of pause, where Justin held his gaze, unblinking, the firelight accentuating every detail of his face. His lips rose on one side into a subtle smile.

Then it was over.

Justin wrinkled his nose and looked away.

Derek forced himself to swallow. The emotion in Justin's eyes contained a hesitant depth of affection Justin had never shown him before, which made asking this next question agonizing.

"Justin, do you mind heading over to Nick's tent for the night?"

"Sure." Justin's shoulder brushed up against Derek's coat as he walked past him. "We can change places tomorrow night."

"Well, that's settled then. I'm going to turn in," Nick said as he rose to his feet and grabbed his flashlight. "I had a late night last night. I'll see you later, Justin."

Justin nodded. "Sure thing."

"So, I guess I'm all alone tonight," Derek said as he pulled another beer from the cooler.

Sam laughed and pounded Derek on the back. "I'm sure you'll survive. One night sleeping alone is *not* going to kill you."

Derek grunted his feigned acceptance of that statement.

There was little chance he was going to sleep *at all* tonight.

Justin crawled into the tent well ahead of Derek and began gathering up his sleeping bag, pillow, and a few articles of warm clothing. Once away from the fire, it became apparent the chill air threatened an intention of dropping much further.

He stopped what he was doing and sunk onto his heels. He'd rather be pressed up against Derek for the night to stay warm. Extra layers of clothing made a poor second choice.

He flipped his pillow over and brought it to his chest.

What Sam had said, about his wanting to fuck Derek, he'd hit it straight on. Almost. He wanted so much more than that from Derek. They'd practically built a life together already.

Together, yes, but apart.

Justin sighed, remembering the day on the bleachers in high school when Derek had asked him if he had feelings for him. He rolled his eyes. He'd been such an idiot in retrospect, but the thought of losing Derek had outweighed everything else that day.

He clutched his pillow closer. At the time, it had seemed denying his feelings was the right move. Derek had come out soon after, and it became obvious Derek was never going to look at him the way he wanted him to anyway. The way he fantasized life might be between them.

Justin sniffed and rubbed his nose. Maybe sleeping so close to Derek tonight would've been awkward after what Sam had implied.

He tossed his pillow aside and resumed his half-blind scramble in the intermittent darkness, his flashlight acting up, providing a light show worthy of a nightclub, flashing in and out of existence. A steady stream of light lit up the interior of the tent.

"Move," Derek mumbled from behind him.

Despite the fact he was kneeling, Justin's legs were barely holding him steady after the quantity of alcohol he'd consumed. Toppling over was inevitable as Derek crowded in against him. He took the opportunity to lie down for a second.

Just until his head stopped spinning.

His plan this weekend was to get mind-numbingly drunk as he did every weekend they all went camping—a coping mechanism he'd employed to lessen his inner torment and stress.

Destructive and nauseating but effective.

Somewhat.

"I think I drank too much," Derek slurred into his pillow.

Justin yawned and threw an arm over his face, hoping the action would stop his head from swimming.

Hardly.

Derek's idea of drinking too much involved consuming less than a six-pack during an entire evening.

"You sounded good tonight," Derek said as he shifted onto his side. "Was that last song one of yours?"

"Mm ...been working on it in my head this past week."

"It's really good."

"Thanks."

Justin clenched his eyes shut. His thoughts suspended somewhere between prayer and hope as he listened to Derek move closer to him. Maybe Sam's rant had stirred something in him.

Don't be a fucking idiot.

Yet his body burgeoned with the dim prospect of Derek's actions when his best friend's hand came to rest on his chest. Strong and heavy, as it had so many times before.

He breathed up into its weight as Derek's thumb stroked the material of his jacket. Deep down, he knew there was no intent beyond friendship, so he bottled the impulse to turn toward Derek, capture his lips, and run his hands through the thick dark curls that were more often than not decorated with drywall dust, wood chips, and colorful stripped casings of electrical wires.

"Hey, about what Sam said ...," Derek mumbled.

"Yeah, what the hell, right?" Justin attempted a laugh but only managed a single exhalation in its place, panic strangling his breath. He hadn't expected Derek to bring up what Sam had said. His breath quickened, fueled by uncertainty.

Derek grunted and laughed, barely audible. "That's our Sam for you."

"Yeah," Justin whispered. "It sure is."

Derek stopped stroking the material of Justin's coat but left his hand where it lay, resting on Justin's chest. He shifted his shoulder and repositioned his pillow. The change in position brought Derek close enough for Justin to feel Derek's warm breath on his cheek.

"Justin."

"Yeah?"

"You like working with me, don't you? The whole business? Our business. Doing renovations and everything." Derek's hand emphasized each sentence in turn by patting Justin's chest.

"Of course, I do." Justin laughed, the sound erupting short and breathy. "Do you honestly think I'd put up with you otherwise?"

"I'd like to think so," Derek said.

Justin laughed in earnest this time. "Yeah, I suppose. Right back at you. Who else would put up with me singing twenty-four seven?"

"But is that ..."

Derek fell silent as he gripped Justin's coat, then smoothed it out.

"Never mind," he mumbled into his pillow.

They must have passed out because Justin found himself being startled awake when Derek coughed, pulled his hand away, and curled up facing away from him.

"You better head over to Nick's tent," Derek said. "I think we fell asleep."

Justin cleared his throat. "Yeah. Right. Sure."

Within moments, he was struggling to gather up his things to share a tent with a man he barely knew, while his body was aching to be held by the one person who'd made it impossible for him to love anyone else. His dream of a wife, a loving home, and children were nothing more than a glimmering illusion. He'd left a string of ex-girlfriends in his wake because of Derek.

Every woman he'd ever had a serious relationship with eventually backed away when it became apparent he wasn't capable of committing to them long-term.

As each year passed, he'd come to accept he'd never have a life similar to his parents. Not while Derek continued to have an unrelenting hold on his heart.

Justin slipped out of the tent, paused for a moment, and looked up at the star-filled sky as he clung tight to his motley collection of belongings.

He snorted through a laugh. Wishing on a shooting star was more likely to grant him a release from Derek's hold on him than the course he was on currently.

"You hear that, star," Justin mumbled, almost dropping his pillow as he spun around staring skyward. "Help me let him go." He stumbled to keep his balance until he slammed up against a tree, his back pressed firmly to its ridged bark, steadying the tilt-a-whirl in his head—the nauseating repercussion of suppressing a steadfast heart intent on inciting an absurd unattainable duet between him and Derek.

Justin kicked at an offshoot of root extending from the tree, unsheathing a small section while swearing under his breath. His feelings toward Derek were never going to relinquish their grip on his life. It was a reality he knew was slowly crushing him.

He grunted in aggravation and took a moment to relieve himself before setting off across the open area surrounding the fire pit. His pillow, sleeping bag, and extra clothes being released, then retrieved. Released—retrieved. Released—retrieved, imitating a pack of rebellious children on a midnight outing, their chaperone too drunk to contain them.

Justin bashed his flashlight against his thigh a few times. It was still acting up, stubbornly refusing to stay lit. He careened onward, undaunted by the obstacle course of discarded beer bottles encircling the fire pit. He stuffed the flashlight into his coat pocket as he arrived fireside.

He stared down at where they'd all been gathered earlier, the warm, cheery glow of the firelight uniting them, now dark and cold.

Justin blinked as he willed his eyes to adjust, then staggered along the gravel road leading to the site where Nick had pitched his tent.

He managed to remain on his feet despite the relative darkness.

Arriving with minimal swearing, he pawed at the billowy fabric until he found the tent flap and unzipped it. He looked back over his shoulder toward the direction of Derek's tent.

Their tent. They'd bought it together.

It was where he should be. Their bodies entwined skin against skin.

Not here.

Justin lowered his chin to rest on his chest.

It'll never be.

Derek had been acting differently though. Nervous almost.

You're drunk.

Go to sleep.

Chapter Four

After edging into the empty space on the tent floor, Justin had kicked his boots off, shrugged out of his coat, and shimmied his way into his sleeping bag when Nick spoke.

"Thanks for doing this for me. I know you'd rather be sleeping with Derek."

With?

Like with, with? Or just with?

Justin rolled over and pushed himself up onto one elbow as his gut twisted, tense with apprehension.

Nick's tone.

He has to be joking.

His ability to make out Nick's features was hindered, given the limited amount of moonlight illuminating the tent. He couldn't be sure without asking.

"What do you mean?" Justin asked.

"I saw the way you were looking at him tonight."

The sound of Nick emitting a short laugh after that statement sent shivers up Justin's spine, prickling his skin. It wasn't a malicious sound necessarily, but it unsettled him. He was Sam's cousin, but Sam hadn't seen him in years, so they didn't know much about him.

"Too bad he's completely oblivious," Nick added as he moved closer to Justin. "He has no idea what he's passing up."

Justin shifted his position and backed away.

There was purpose in Nick's advance.

Obvious purpose.

"Whoa, Nick." Justin raised his hand and pressed it against Nick's bare chest. "I think you've got me all wrong."

"Do I?" Nick snatched Justin's hand from his chest, restraining it, and guided it down his body.

Justin groaned as his hand was thrust into the front of Nick's sweatpants and introduced to Nick's semi-erect cock. He didn't retreat or recoil.

He should have, but he didn't. Likely, due to the excessive amount of alcohol he'd consumed, but maybe not. Inebriation aside, he should have stopped himself from wrapping his fingers around Nick's thick girth, and caressing its warmth, but he didn't.

"Okay," Justin admitted. "Maybe not entirely wrong."

"Thought so," Nick said, then released Justin's arm to grapple him closer.

Whoa, hold on.

Justin whipped his hand out from the front of Nick's sweatpants. "I'm not going to sleep with you."

"Why not?" Nick asked. His movements were ardent and determined as he unzipped his sleeping bag and shrugged out of his sweatpants, and tossed them behind him.

"No." Justin shifted his body until he felt the material of the tent wall straining behind him. He was unable to back up any further.

He shivered as a gust of chill air rushed past the exterior of the tent, permeating his spine and radiating its indifference to his situation, straight through to his chest.

He clenched his hands into fists—prepared.

"Come on," Nick said. "You know you want to."

"Nick, stop," Justin almost shouted as a rough hand fumbled and narrowly succeeded in unzipping the entirety of his sleeping bag.

Justin reached for the zipper, wanting to re-encase himself against the threat but missed, grazing his knuckles on the sharp metal teeth before making contact with Nick's arm.

"I'm serious. I'm not interested," Justin said, shoving Nick to push him away, but Nick held steadfast, his much larger frame making him immovable.

"Come on. I know you've been working hard all week," Nick persisted as he stroked the back of his hand up and down the front of Justin's sweatshirt.

A soft exhalation and unmistakable sigh of arousal escaped Justin's lips as Nick's fingers found his taut nipple through the material, and pinched it, teasing it.

"See," Nick said. "You deserve a little attention."

"Nick, I don't want—"

"All right." Nick's urgency subsided, but he didn't appear to be giving up. He retained the closeness of their bodies. "I wanted to tell you that when we were making our way back to camp, you were great. You didn't push me for details. I appreciate that."

Justin shrugged. "I figured you'd tell me what you felt comfortable sharing."

"Still." There was a brief silence before Nick spoke again. "Justin, I …" He scrubbed a hand down the side of his face. "This is crazy. And I don't know where it's coming from, but I've never wanted to be with a guy before, you know …until I met you." Nick smirked through a quiet laugh. "I get it though if you're not interested in doing anything with me."

"That's not necessarily true, but I don't feel comfortable with us hooking up."

"Okay, but could I kiss you at least?" Nick licked his lips. "That's it, I promise. I need to know if I'm imagining things."

Justin's mind flipped through what seemed a million scenarios. Maybe Nick would be satisfied with this one concession and leave him alone.

Then he could slip back over to Derek's tent.

Run back to Derek?

Why?

A ripple of indecision invaded his resolve, driven by need.

Maybe playing around with Nick wasn't such a big deal.

Justin grasped Nick's face and guided him toward his mouth,

encouraging Nick to layer his body atop his own. His tongue slipped between Nick's soft, moist lips and he lapped at the erotic combination of saliva and desire. It had been a while since he'd fooled around with a guy, his latest ex-girlfriend occupying the last two years of his life.

His body was going to want much more than a kiss. Watching Derek split logs all afternoon had primed his body for a bit of male attention.

Justin's thoughts lingered on Derek, and his body warmed, remembering the closeness of Derek's to his own. Tucked so close to him they may as well have been in the same sleeping bag.

His body vibrated, arousal overtaking his inhibitions.

"If we take it further, you won't say anything?" Justin said.

"I promise," Nick replied as he smiled against Justin's lips. "No one will ever know."

Justin's deepest concern bubbled up and surfaced, addressed. This was a part of his life he preferred to keep private. He'd kept his sexuality a secret for so many years now he wasn't sure how his friends and family would react. It hadn't been intentional, but when Derek had come out, he'd buried himself deeper in the closet, not wanting their friendship to become awkward.

He pinched his eyes closed. He knew sleeping with Sam's cousin was crossing the line, but right now, he didn't care. "Absolutely no one," he emphasized.

"Trust me," Nick replied. "I don't want anyone to know about this either."

Justin cleared his mind of the risks, accepting Nick's assurances, and wrapped his arms around Nick's body, caressing the bulky muscles of his shoulders.

"Nick, I don't do everything."

He groaned as Nick's hardened cock ground against his own, tempting him to reconsider. He wasn't opposed to *going all the way*, but for now, he was strictly a handjob, blowjob, frottage kind of guy. Unless, of course, he found himself in bed with the right guy.

Never going to happen, Leary.

Let it go.

"I was kind of hoping you'd fuck me," Nick replied, then shrugged. "But whatever works for you. I have no idea what I'm doing anyway."

Justin smirked.

You want me to fuck you.

Yeah, right.

This *was not* Nick's first time.

Justin forced Nick onto his back, straddled his thighs, and stripped his sweatshirt up over his head, discarding it. Despite the cold, he was overheating.

Nick lay breathless beneath him, aroused, wanting.

At least he wants me.

Justin stood, shimmied the sweatpants off his hips, and pushed them down around his ankles.

Nick hummed as he brushed his hands up Justin's chest, furrowing his fingers into the light offering of hair as Justin rested back atop him.

"Come closer." Nick hauled on Justin's hips. "I want to gag on that beautiful cock of yours."

Justin grunted with exhilaration.

Definitely not his first time.

"Move down a bit," he said and positioned Nick closer to the center of the tent, so he'd have enough room to place his hands on the ground.

He smirked when Nick nudged him, directing him to pin his arms down.

Whatever you want, sweetheart.

Justin wrapped his hands around Nick's wrists and held them restrained against the floor of the tent before descending. He slid his cock between Nick's full, wet lips. Lips he'd been kissing mere moments before. Warm and hungry, caressing his length.

Yeah, there.

Good boy.

Thrusting his cock deeper into Nick's throat, Nick began making the most amazing sounds. A rumbling combination of distress and enjoyment, revving up his aggressive side. Justin drilled the man beneath him to the point of gagging and coughing.

He sneered as he looked down, catching glimpses of his cock sliding back and forth into Nick's mouth in the faint moonlight, his chin, and lips coated in saliva and mucus.

"Fuck yeah, bitch," Justin whispered. "Take it all."

Nick's gut rose in what felt like a laugh, and then his knees came up against Justin's ass. He rolled Justin's body off his own and onto the tent floor.

The floor was cold and hard against Justin's back. He struggled to right himself, but his pants, now twisted around his ankles, were impeding his ability to maneuver effectively.

"Hands and knees," Nick said. "I want to taste your ass."

Justin faltered. "But I've never—"

"Me either," Nick said, dismissing Justin's apprehension. "I want to taste you ...really get my tongue in there. Then I'll go back to sucking you off."

Damn, he really has done this before.

Hardcore.

Justin shook his head. "No, I—"

"Come on, Justin."

"Nick, I said no."

Justin reached for the waistband of his sweatpants and tried to drag them back into place, but Nick was on him, flipping him over onto his chest, and breaking Justin's grip of the fabric.

Nick's hot breath rushed past his ear.

"I said on your knees ...*bitch*."

"Fuck off." Justin struggled to jam his elbow into Nick's body, but Nick was packed tight against his back. He wasn't able to gain enough space to oust him. "I mean it. Get the fuck off."

A low, unsettling laugh from above reverberated through to his gut.

Fucking asshole.

"Get off." Justin struggled upward again, grunting with the effort required to shift the weight of Nick's body off his own. He managed to move his arms until they were beneath him.

He pressed himself up off the tent floor, at last managing to extend his arms fully. If he could maneuver his legs under him, he'd be able to crouch, throw Nick off, and escape the tent.

Nick grabbed a handful of his hair, wrenched it within his fist, and shoved Justin's face back toward the ground.

Justin grunted and released a near silent string of obscenities as his shoulders burned to support him, but the force of Nick's weight eventually shot his arms out from beneath him.

His chest collided with the floor of the tent, winding him. He struggled to break free, but Nick's massive palm smothered the side of his face, pressing him further into the bedding.

The dank, musty smell of a sleeping bag, stored damp too many times over the years, flooded his senses. He held his jaw together tight. He needed to stay quiet. The embarrassment of being overheard would be devastating.

He should never have agreed to this.

The head of Nick's hard cock jabbed the flesh between his thighs.

Oh, fuck no!

His heart thundered, screaming with comprehension. Up until then, it hadn't occurred to him what was happening.

"Nick, stop." His voice came out muffled, the fabric of his sleeping bag barely fluttering beneath his lips.

"Shut up," Nick whispered, his rasping breath hissing across the surface of Justin's cheek. "You shut the fuck up. Or Derek and everyone else will hear you."

I know—

Justin clenched his muscles in futile desperation as one of

his legs was thrust away from its partner, a barrier he'd been hoping to maintain.

Nick forced his way forward.

Jamming. Prodding.

Oh, God, no.

"Stay still you little *bitch*," Nick grunted. "You know you want it."

God, no. No, I don't ...please.

"Nick. No. Please ..."

Panic swelled in his chest.

No, no, no—

Oh, God—

Justin shut his eyes as Nick's unsheathed, unlubed cock drove straight into his gut. His only objection, a smothered cry, and high-pitched whimper. A sound that only served to encourage the grunting mass atop him.

He sucked in a wet quivering gasp.

Popping, crackling light.

—Searing.

Burning pain.

—Revulsion.

Panic.

Breathe.

Nick slammed his hips against Justin's ass, his thick fingers digging into Justin's flesh as he drove his cock deeper.

The burn intensified.

He knew he needed to relax, but his body refused to listen.

"Nick, —please. Please ..."

"That's it, *bitch*. Beg for it."

Scorching tendrils of agony bolted up Justin's spine, dipping his world into a moment of complete darkness. He could have stayed there, but...

No...

"That's the way you like it, isn't it?" Nick continued. "Hard and fast up the ass, you fucking faggot."

"Stop," Justin groaned, but his voice was shrouded by the thick down sleeping bag he'd insisted on bringing for added warmth. "I'm not. I don't want ..."

He pinched his eyes shut as a hot rush of tears escaped.

Oh, God, no.

His cock hardened beneath his stomach, then pulsed, wave after wave, slicking up the material beneath him, horrifying him. He hadn't been able to stop it.

Justin convulsed through a series of sobs, saliva, and snot coating his sputtering lips, the embarrassment, and frenetic denial, pumping air in and out of his lungs in shuddering gasps.

Blistering surges of heat.

His neck, his face. Burning.

He released a soft breath and shut his eyes, blocking out everything, but the sounds of the forest.

Tree debris *...tick, tick, tick* ...dropping onto the tent.

Qua, qua, qua.

A raven. Directly above.

Scolding.

Don't you dare ...you have no idea.

Qua, qua, qua.

No, it was encouragement. Not scolding.

Justin twisted his arms, his wrists burning, churning, and fighting.

—the hold, released.

Freed, Justin reached out, seeking, searching for anything substantial. A weapon.

It's too dark to see anything.

He patted the ground in frantic sweeps.

—there's nothing.

He slammed his hands on the ground.

Get off!

He reached back, scratching at Nick's thighs, tearing at his flesh, struggling to stop him, but Nick was built like a truck, pinning him down. He had no chance of getting out from under him.

God, stop!

Please, please stop.

Justin moaned as Nick's hot sweaty breath buffeted his cheek from behind. Gust after foul gust, dampening his skin. His own breath forced from his lungs, again ...and again ...and again, his chest battered, crushed against the unfeeling earth beneath him.

Rocking, rhythmic pain. Incredible.

Electrifying his flesh. Numbing his thoughts.

It was too much.

Qua, qua, qua...

The flutter of wings. Freedom.

...peace.

He slipped into silence, surrendering, defeated ...lifeless, prompting Nick to drive into him harder.

Fresh sparks of agony lit up the darkness behind Justin's eyes, but he took it with nothing more than an exhalation.

Finish ...please finish.

...the comforting scent of wood smoke ...lingering.

...wind caressing the trees overhead, swishing ...rustling.

Indifferent.

—*I can't cry out.*

He closed his eyes tight.

—*Can't.*

Justin reached out and touched the cool fabric of the tent, then stroked his fingers along it, fascinated by its normality.

...spatters of rain, *spat-spat-spat*, overhead.

Keeping time like a metronome.

Time that seemed to go on forever.

The bile rose in Justin's throat. He felt himself being torn up inside by the thick blunt head of Nick's cock. His unsheathed cock.

Hell no. This has to stop.

Justin thrust his hips back and struggled with everything he had left, squirming furiously to get away, but that pissed Nick off, and he compressed Justin's face further into the sleeping bag.

Stop! Can't breathe!

Justin flung his arms back, sweeping around behind him, trying to break Nick's connection with his face, but his efforts were useless. Nick was unyielding.

The sleeping bag rattled against his nostrils as he tried to draw breath. Time after time, the air seeped from his lungs, burning to take in more than had been expelled.

Popping, dancing, colored dots.

That's it.

I'm done.

Buzzing. Darkness.

Derek.

He needed Derek like he'd never needed him before. Justin concentrated on reaching his mouth with his hand so he could compress the sleeping bag enough to draw in a slim breath.

A cold waft of air greeted his nostrils. He sucked in the pool of saliva and perspiration coating his face as he took a breath.

He fought the nausea rising in his throat before calling out.

"Derek!"

It didn't even sound like his voice.

…and it wasn't near loud enough.

He coughed and gasped to fill his lungs, properly this time, and put all his effort into yelling. He didn't stop screaming Derek's name until he heard voices calling his own.

Chapter Five

Justin's head slammed against the tent floor, Nick's hand restraining it in place, accompanied by a thick guttural swath of profanities as Nick pulled out, tearing Justin's flesh further.

Then complete chaos.

The sound of the tent's flap being torn away.

Someone shouting his name.

The darkness of the tent filling with streaks of flashlight illumination.

More shouting.

Anger …so much anger.

Someone shouting at Nick to stop running.

Then a cold blast of air rolled over him.

Justin scrambled to the edge of the tent, his sleeping bag gathered around him. Someone had poked their head into the tent, but now they were gone.

He covered his ears, not wanting to hear the brutal sounds of retribution being exacted beyond the tent walls, thankful the thundering beat of his heart blocked most of it out.

Stop.

Please stop.

Trembling. Justin's only escape, rocking. Rocking and chanting *no* beneath his breath. He tried to remove himself from the reality of what had happened.

Was happening.

Happening.

Karen's voice broke through, and Justin scurried to cover himself more thoroughly. He yanked his pants back onto his hips.

He'd never felt so humiliated in his life.

He cowered in the corner of the tent as Karen crept closer, a small flashlight streaking light everywhere, exposing his shame.

"Justin?" Karen scanned the darkness. "Are you all right?"

Justin shook his head and brought his hands up to cover his face. "I …please …" His life may as well be over. And he wanted to be left alone.

Then there was silence.

Glorious silence.

He wasn't sure how much time passed before he jumped, the sound of a car door slamming beyond the tent startling him.

"It's the police," Karen said.

Justin shuddered through a sob.

No.

Please, please, no.

Karen moved closer and set her flashlight down on the sleeping bag, illuminating its tainted surface. She reached for Justin, moving to grasp his shoulder, but Justin jerked away before she made contact. She retreated, covered her mouth, and sucked in a breath past her fingers.

"Jeez, Justin …you're bleeding."

Justin didn't hear anything after that. His mind had succumbed to a place of glorious numbness, escaping from the nightmare that continued to descend upon him.

The smoke drifted above their heads then parted, the wind pulling and dividing it until its ghostly presence disappeared.

Justin relaxed, stretched his legs out, and folded an arm behind his head as he glanced over at Derek. The cigarette passed easily between them.

The break had been unexpected, but until the electrician arrived to complete his work, they were free to take a few minutes.

Derek's heavy work boot came to rest against his, tapping it a few times. There was no question or observation attached to the gesture, but a physical, "Hey." It would continue until he reciprocated. A ritual they'd fallen into over the years.

Justin scratched his head, ruffling his hair, and continued staring up at the burgeoning, spring leaves of the tree they were lying beneath in comfortable stillness.

He took the cigarette offered, lingering for a moment as their hands connected. It was never to be ...him and Derek, but this silent exchange between them would be enough to fuel him for another day. There was a connection between them that could never be broken.

Karen placed her hands on the tent floor, close enough to Justin to catch his attention without touching him. "Sweetheart, everything is going to be all right. Sam and Derek are talking to the police. Let's get you dressed, so you can speak with them, okay?"

She reached for a discarded shirt, but Justin batted it away, snapping out of his stupor.

"Fuck no. That's his." Justin jutted his chin in the direction of his own shirt. "Mine is over there."

Karen lifted the rumpled sweatshirt and turned it right side out.

"Do you want to tell me what happened?" she asked as she handed Justin his shirt. "Did he jump you?"

Justin avoided her gaze. "No."

"Justin, the police want to speak with you," Sam interrupted as he poked his head into the tent. "They need a statement."

He grabbed Nick's shirt and sweatpants when Karen handed them up to him.

"Tell them to go," Justin replied. "I'm not pressing charges."

"Justin, you have to."

"Why?" Justin stared at Karen. "Nothing happened."

Sam crawled further into the tent. "Don't be ridiculous. Derek was the first one to get here. He saw what was going on. He saw you lying there—"

Justin turned away, wrapping his arms around his body as if doing so would somehow protect him from further humiliation.

It wasn't helping.

"It was my fault." He swiped a hand under his nose. It was running like a son of a bitch.

Bitch.

Justin scrubbed a hand across his face.

I asked for it.

I reached for him ...I kissed him.

He shuddered.

I fucked his face and called him my bitch.

Fuck.

"I think we got carried away," Justin said.

"Are you kidding me? I beat the crap out of my cousin," Sam shouted, "and had the park attendant call the police because you panicked during rough sex. Seriously? What the fuck?"

Justin ignored Sam and picked at the zipper of his sleeping bag. Anything to keep from looking in the direction of the torn opening of the tent where Derek had appeared.

He didn't want to see the disgust on Derek's face.

He'd let a meaningless guy ride him bareback, and Derek had seen enough to know that.

"Guys, give us a minute," Derek asked Sam and Karen.

Justin gathered the sleeping bag closer.

Please, no.

As the tent emptied, Derek made his way inside and sat cross-legged across from Justin on the bare tent floor. "Hey, buddy. How are you doing?"

Justin folded the sleeping bag over and pushed it into a corner, to keep Derek from seeing the slick, bloody mess on it. "I don't want to talk about it. Just get me out of here. Please."

"What about the police? You should—"

"Derek, no ...please."

Justin refused to make eye contact with Derek, occupying

himself with a study of the tent floor instead, as he attempted to wipe away the mess on his face with a tissue Derek had handed him.

This is it.

Their time together was done.

He'd heard it in Derek's voice …sensed it in his body language.

He'd never be able to lose himself in Derek's warm, seductive eyes ever again.

He'd never again embrace his laughter.

Breathe up into his touch.

Never.

They were done.

"All right," Derek said as he prepared to exit the tent. "I'll get rid of the cops and take you home."

Justin nodded, pulled his knees up, and hugged them close to his body. A tear trickled down his cheek. He'd never felt more like dying than he did right then.

Chapter Six

The ride back into town was quiet, solemn. Derek decided against listening to the radio in case Justin wanted to talk. He didn't utter a word, but he wanted to leave that option open. Even though he wasn't sure what he would say in response to anything Justin decided to share.

He would've been at a loss.

His best friend had lied to him about something so incredibly fundamental it might have changed the course of their entire relationship. It might have changed the course of what had unfolded tonight.

Maybe if he'd known Justin was gay, he would have paid more attention to the interactions between Nick and Justin. Maybe he could have spotted something in Nick.

A darker side.

Maybe.

Derek leaned his head back against the headrest, attempting to draw some solace from its support. Throughout the years they'd spent together, practically every waking moment, Justin had never thought to mention he was attracted to guys.

Even after he'd come out himself.

Nothing.

His breath caught, quickening, then he released it, praying Justin wouldn't notice the low, anguished sound he hadn't managed to subdue. According to Karen, what he'd seen. Justin stripped bare, his sweatpants tangled around his ankles, face down on the tent floor sobbing, had started consensually.

He peered over at Justin and smeared a wet shield of tears from his eyelashes with the heel of his hand. Justin had sought the company of a guy he barely knew instead of him.

Derek pressed his eyes shut for the briefest of moments, willing his stomach to retain its contents. He was close to vomiting.

Breathe.

He fixed his eyes back on the road and cracked his window open a fraction, then turned down a gravel road. His headlights offered the only illumination in a neighborhood where the homes were set back into the wooded area, making them invisible from the road.

"Justin, I—"

And what the hell are you going to say? Justin, I'm sorry you ended up in Nick's tent. I'm sorry I've never told you how much I love you...

His breath shuddered as it escaped. Regret filling his chest. The look Justin leveled at him from across the truck's cab as he spoke his name, was mired deep in anguish.

If only I could reach out.

"We should take you to the hospital," Derek said, modifying what he'd started to say. "Karen said she saw—"

Damn it.

Derek gripped tight to the steering wheel.

It needs to be said.

"Are you in any pain?" he asked. "Because if you have any sharp pains down there, you need to tell me." He shifted in his seat, attempting to quell his stomach. "There's medication now for ...right after, in case of HIV. I, um, didn't see a condom. Did he use one?"

Justin didn't respond, instead tucking his face against the passenger window, his hand poised on the door handle as Derek pulled up to Justin's house.

"Thanks for the ride—" Justin mumbled as he flung the door open.

"Whoa, hold up." Derek shut the truck off and raced around

to the passenger side. He backed away when it looked as though Justin's annoyance was escalating to the point of hitting him.

"I'm going to stick around until you get settled," Derek said.

Justin pushed past him. "Suit yourself."

"Thank you. I will."

Derek followed behind, crossing and uncrossing his arms to stop himself from helping Justin climb the front steps. He took the keys Justin was fumbling against the lock and let them into the house they'd built together, many years ago on land Justin's granny had gifted him.

The laughs they'd had designing and building the entire house, seemed distant memories. Now the front entry was cold and dark, adding to the silent discomfort hovering between them, the depth of which Derek had only encountered once before.

He cleared his mind of it. It was in the past. The life he'd briefly shared a sliver of time with had only brought him pain. Pain and regret.

So much regret.

Derek grabbed the banister at the base of the stairs, letting Justin pass by him. Outside, Justin had barely made it up the front steps, so he followed Justin up to the bathroom and attempted to steer him away from washing evidence away. He'd been hoping to convince Justin to go to the hospital and have a rape kit done, despite having driven him home.

His advice was met with violent resistance, and once they stepped into the bathroom, Justin almost took a swing at him. In earnest this time.

Derek took a few steps back as Justin sunk to his knees on the bathroom floor, attempting to force gasps of air past an eruption of silent, convulsive sobbing.

"Justin, please—," Derek whispered.

Justin smeared the tears off his face.

"It wasn't like that," he said. "Things got out of hand. That's it." He wrapped his arms around his head, staring down at the tiles on the floor as he rocked back and forth.

"Then why are you ...?" Derek reached for Justin, then withdrew. "Justin, if you're in pain, you need to be looked at. Seriously, please. Let me take you to the hospital."

Justin lowered his arms and glared at Derek as he clambered up off the bathroom floor. "Drop it, Derek. I mean it. Or I will drop *you* like a fucking stone in here."

"Fine." Derek reached into the tub enclosure and turned the water on. The ornate taps Justin had insisted on buying were loose, making controlling the temperature difficult.

He was surprised Justin hadn't fixed them.

That isn't like him.

"First thing tomorrow, I'm going to call Sam," Derek said, peering back over his shoulder. "I want to make sure Nick has left town since you're not planning on pressing charges."

Justin shrugged and sunk onto the toilet seat.

"Whatever," he replied.

Derek almost released a sigh of relief as the discussion reached its conclusion. He wasn't going to push his suggestions any further. The truth—Justin's decision to avoid the hospital suited him fine even though it ran in the face of every logical reason to the contrary.

He rose to lean against the counter, recalling the cruel repugnant treatment that had been doled out by the emergency staff, as he'd stood helpless. Speechless. Enraged to the point of silence so many years ago. He wrapped his arms around his waist, screaming inside.

The regret resurfacing. The memory prickling Derek's skin.

He'd done nothing.

Absolutely nothing.

He'd stood there as simple human compassion was consumed by judgment and righteousness. Not even love had moved him to act.

Coward.

"Get out," Justin shouted as he stood from his perch on the edge of the toilet seat, his face flushed, his fists clenched.

Derek moved toward the door but paused to stare at the deepening purple bruise on one of Justin's wrists. Nick must have restrained him at some point. To what extent, he wasn't sure.

He brushed a thumb back and forth across the crook of his forefinger, focusing on the callous there. In the truck, he'd almost reached out to caress Justin's discolored flesh with his fingers, in an attempt to soothe and repair the damage.

"Are you going to be all right?" Derek asked.

"I've taken showers before asshole."

Justin shoved Derek hard, knocking him backward, his angry fists pounding Derek out into the hall.

The door slammed shut.

Derek grunted and sunk to the floor outside the bathroom door, dropping his head back against the wall. He twisted around, listening.

Fuck, he's crying again.

He closed his eyes and concentrated on the sound of the shower instead until it was the only sound coming from beyond the door. The image of Justin face down on the floor of the tent resurfaced. Screaming. Helpless. Violated.

He tried to block it out but couldn't.

It would be forever imprinted on his mind.

A shiver ran through him.

Justin would still be carrying Nick's scent on his skin.

On his lips.

On his smile.

Derek ruffled Justin's summer bleached hair as he darted past to take a seat beside him. Justin's mom had brought home their favorite ice cream bars, and they were melting fast.

"You're telling me you've never kissed anyone," he asked Justin, repeating a question he'd asked as they were dashing

toward the house after seeing Justin's mom return.

Justin shook his head.

"Why not?" Derek interrogated further.

Justin shrugged. "Just because."

Derek tipped his head to one side, studying the accumulation of ice cream coating Justin's lips.

He wrinkled his nose and sighed.

Justin peered over at him. "Have you?"

"Sure," Derek answered. "Tons."

"Oh—"

Derek sucked at the smear of chocolate coating his knuckle, hoping Justin wouldn't catch on to the fact he was lying.

He glanced up as Justin leaped from his seat, dropped his ice cream, and bolted for the house.

Derek cracked his head back against the wall as a surge of regret bubbled up. That had been the summer before he'd asked Justin if he had feelings for him.

He'd received his answer that day and moved on.

No, you didn't.

Not quietly anyway.

"What about her?" Derek pointed across the crowded cafeteria toward a girl who was in his and Justin's biology class. "She's always turning around and looking at you in class."

"Yeah, right." Justin elbowed Derek, making him drop his apple onto the floor. "She's probably looking at you."

"No way. Not possible." Derek grinned. "Well, maybe." He took a bite of his sandwich, disregarding the errant apple as he perused the room. "It's a well-known fact that hot girls go for the bad boys."

Justin snorted, laughing. "Lawrence, did you just refer to yourself as a bad boy?"

Derek shrugged, then nudged Justin's arm.

"Okay, what about her?" Derek asked.

Justin shook his head. "Nah. Not my type."

"Her?"

"No." Justin stuffed the thermos he'd been drinking from into his backpack. "You can stop now."

"Oh. Her." Derek poked Justin's shoulder. "Her, right?"

"No." The remainder of Derek's lunch ended up on the floor as Justin pushed him aside to untangle himself from the cafeteria's picnic table style seating. "Cut it out. I mean it."

"What?" Derek escaped the table and chased after Justin. "I'm just looking out for you, buddy. Don't you want to get laid?"

Justin turned on Derek and knocked him into the lockers. "What the hell has gotten into you? Suddenly my love life is so damn interesting to you?"

"I don't understand why you're so upset. Can't a guy look out for his best friend?"

"Yeah, but—"

"Yeah, but what?"

He'd been convinced Justin wasn't being honest with him. And he'd been relentless, challenging Justin at every opportunity. Pushing him to *confess.*

Pushing Justin to confess he was in love with him.

Derek wrinkled his brow and checked his phone. It was only four-thirty in the morning. He rubbed a tired hand across his face after paging through his text messages.

"Only nine messages from Karen," he mumbled to himself. "Impressive restraint." He opened and closed the text thread a few times, not convinced he wanted to encourage her by answering. He decided against engaging in a conversation with her. He could call her once he had Justin settled.

The next unanswered text message wasn't as easy to ignore. Derek tapped the edge of the screen with his thumb, the name

Breanne Leary staring up at him.

Subject line, "Hey sweetness."

He flicked open the message. Justin's sister, Breanne, was coming into town for a few days and was hoping to meet up with everyone.

Derek returned the phone to his coat pocket. Seven years and not a single word from her until tonight. "You're timing sucks, Bree."

Seven whole years. He'd begun to think Breanne had forgotten she had a brother. And there was his own relationship with her as well. After all the heartache they'd been through together, she'd run off and left him to suffer through the loss. Alone. It was one of the few times he'd kept part of his life secret from Justin. From everyone. Everyone, except Breanne …and she'd abandoned him.

Derek reached over and tapped on the door, eyes closed as he waited. Thirty minutes had passed since he'd been ousted from the bathroom.

"I'm going to make some tea." He reached up and tried the handle when Justin didn't answer.

It was locked. And the bathroom was far *too* quiet.

"Justin!" Derek jumped to his feet and pounded at the solid obtrusive barrier blocking him from where he needed to be. "Justin, answer me!"

Panic surged up into his chest.

This isn't happening.

"Justin! Unlock this fucking door!"

Still, no answer.

Derek stepped back, tucked his arms across his chest, and crashed into the door, splintering a large section, but the latch continued to hold. He pressed against the shattered door, the damage significant enough for him to catch sight of Justin sitting in the bottom of the tub.

He wasn't moving.

Jesus Christ, Justin.

He ran at the door, brutalizing his shoulder with every attempt, until the latch finally snapped free, breaking loose of the frame.

Derek's legs propelled him to the edge of the tub, and he crashed to the floor. He pressed his fingers to Justin's throat, searching for a pulse.

Faint. Way too faint.

He scanned the room as he dialed 9-1-1.

"Yes, it's an emergency." Derek shut the water off and yanked a towel from the nearest rack to cover Justin. "Ambulance."

"My friend. He's taken some pills." He crawled across the floor to retrieve the bottle. "I have it. Lorazepam." He looked over at Justin. "No, he's not responding."

Derek sunk back onto the floor. "Five-eleven Rosedale." He hadn't known Justin was taking medication. He should have known something like that. "Justin Leary. March fourteen, eighty-five. Yes, I'll stay on the line." He leaned against the tub and stroked Justin's face.

"Stay with me, buddy. I'm right here."

He brushed a thumb across Justin's pale lips.

They were so cold.

Don't you dare leave me.

Chapter Seven

The feel of something tucked into Justin's hand confused him. He squeezed its warmth, trying to determine what it was, but it was immediately pulled away. He considered reaching out, but even the thought of moving his arm tired him.

He began to drift off. It wasn't time to wake up yet. He hadn't heard his alarm.

Oh, come on. What the hell?

Justin groaned as a light flicked on above him. It shone straight through his eyelids, creating an irritating pink glow.

"Hey," a deep, gentle voice rumbled above him. A familiar voice, smooth as honey, then the warm object was in his hand again.

Justin tried to speak, but his lips refused to part. He pushed at them with his tongue, attempting to pry them open. Failing, he relaxed, sinking back away.

If it were important, someone would wake him up.

"Justin."

Derek?

He opened his eyes.

What is Derek doing in my bedroom?

I must have slept in.

He turned his head. Derek's stance at his bedside was odd. He pulled his lips in to wet them until they eventually relinquished their seal.

"Hey," he croaked. "What are you doing here?"

Derek laughed as he leaned closer.

"Waiting for you to wake up," he said.

Justin tensed as he realized it was Derek's hand he was

gripping. He thought about pulling away but decided to leave it there. He hoped Derek wouldn't think it was too weird.

He wrinkled his nose.

Why would he? It had been Derek who'd taken his hand in the first place.

"Still tired," Justin said. "I'll get up later."

"You don't need any more sleep," Derek replied as he brushed his thumb back and forth across the top of Justin's hand.

The gentle nature of Derek's touch sent tingles up Justin's spine. He moved to shift his weight so he could see Derek better, but searing pain rocketed up through his gut. His free hand shot out, clawing around for anything to support himself so the pain would stop.

"Whoa, I've got you." Derek gripped tight to Justin's hand and helped him settle back. He rearranged Justin's pillows to better support his head.

"Just take it easy until a doctor clears you," he said.

"What?" Justin looked around. "Why am I in the hospital?"

"You've been in a coma, buddy. Three days now."

What?

Justin squeezed his eyes shut.

The pills.

The pain. The rape.

Justin's brow dipped, his eyes became glassy, and he turned his face into his pillow.

What is Derek doing here with me?

He ripped his hand away from Derek's grasp.

Murmurs were coming from behind him, Derek and someone else. He sensed someone standing at the far side of his bed. He blinked a few times and exhaled a relaxed breath as a comforting warmth descended upon him.

Justin reached for Derek's arm.

"Derek ..."

"I'm right here," Derek answered.

Justin opened his eyes as Derek's soft breath whispered past his lips.

Yeah, he really is ...right here.

Derek's face was less than an inch away from his own. He held tight to Derek's shoulder, tipped his head back enough to bridge the distance, and touched his lips to Derek's, his own dry, scratchy ones pressing for a brief moment against Derek's supple, moist ones.

Fuck that feels good.

Derek chuckled above him.

"Well, you seem to be feeling better," Derek said as he played with the damp strands of Justin's hair. "I'll be able to bust you out of here before the week is out."

"Derek?"

"Yeah, buddy. What do you need?"

"I need to tell you I love you." Justin's breath caught briefly. "I'm in love with you."

He released his grip on Derek, contented in the fact that Derek had been watching over him as he slept. The man he loved had stayed by his side.

For the moment as he succumbed to sleep, he felt at peace.

"Hurry up," Derek shouted at Justin, who was struggling to carry the assortment of camping gear he'd finally convinced his parents to buy. The thought of him going off into the woods for a weekend of camping had set Justin's mom's already prominent anxiety into overdrive, with images of him being ripped to shreds by bears, or drowning in the lake they were planning on fishing.

"Yeah, yeah," Justin replied and tossed the troublesome armload of equipment into the back of Derek's crappy old pickup truck. He slipped into the passenger seat as Derek revved the engine, his best friend impatient to get started so he could leave his world behind—a world in opposition to the loving, supportive family Justin hadn't appreciated until he'd met Derek.

He'd ignored Derek's request to never come by his house, but they'd been running late if they were going to catch the movie they'd planned on seeing. Derek hadn't shown up to pick him up on time, and he wasn't answering his phone, so he'd ridden his bike to Derek's.

Derek's front door had opened onto a scene of absolute chaos. Justin had almost taken off back home, but Derek had insisted he come in ...that he'd only be a second.

Derek's mom had seemed all right. Despite her obvious addiction to the vodka and cigarettes she'd surrounded herself with, you could tell she loved her son. Derek's step-dad though. The level of hatred aimed at both Derek and his mom had been chilling.

Derek pushed a map at him. "Can you navigate for me?"

"Sure."

Justin smoothed the map open on his lap, located their starting position and destination, and traced the straightforward route with his finger to be sure. They'd picked a campground not too far away, in case they absolutely hated it and wanted to come home.

"Am I coming to the turn-off soon," Derek asked, touching Justin's shoulder.

Justin blinked. "Um, yeah, very soon."

A few miles later, they were pulling into a campground, and finding a campsite amongst a shady grove of massive cedar trees.

Justin stirred, rubbed his eyes, and opened them. It was dark in the room, but he could see the outline of the empty chair across the room without much effort. He pressed his eyes closed.

He should have known better than to hope it would be occupied.

The surrounding area was pitch black, mocking the attempt of their camping lantern to provide any proper light. Derek and Justin stumbled into their tent, laughing, and crawled in the direction of their sleeping bags, and wriggled into them.

Settled in, Justin stared up at the moderate illumination of the tent fabric, sighed with satisfaction, and turned to face Derek.

Derek's face was a hair's breadth from his own.

Unmoving, they stared at each other for what seemed an eternity to Justin, their breath mingling and creating a heated space between them.

Justin blinked when Derek licked his lips. Then Derek rolled away from him, presenting Justin with his broad sweater-clad back.

Sleep did not come easy, the sound of Derek breathing as he slept so close to him, disturbing his ability to relax.

It must've descended on him eventually because as the sun crested the tree line, creating shimmering beams of light that cut straight through the thin fabric of the tent, Justin awoke, his arm draped over Derek's sleeping form.

He made to remove it, but Derek mumbled something, and leaned back against him, indicating in Justin's mind that Derek didn't want to break the embrace.

While envisioning the possibilities, his heart strengthened its thrum, beating at his ribcage, threatening to give away his feelings for Derek. Feelings that had been growing, unchecked, and agonizingly unrequited.

"Damn it's cold," Derek said as he hauled his sleeping bag further up onto his shoulders, forcing Justin to lift his arm away.

Justin blushed as he tucked his arm against his chest. His cheeks warmed despite the cold as he chastised himself for considering the possibility that Derek had been all right with the closeness of their bodies.

Chapter Eight

The drive home seemed longer than usual to Derek. The twists and turns through the dark, densely treed road, echoed the uncertainty creating chaos in his mind. Except he knew this road. Could have driven it with his eyes closed. There should have been no confusion.

Yet, there it was.

He slowed as he passed Justin's driveway, the familiar house nestled deep amongst the trees. Dark. Empty. Not the warm, lively space Justin's presence always created within it.

Derek backed his truck up and turned down Justin's driveway. He rolled to a stop at the base of the front steps, switched the engine off, and watched the last vestiges of sunlight recede behind the roofline before he climbed out of the truck's cab.

It only took a moment to find the key to Justin's house.

It was on his keyring next to his own.

After flicking on a few lights, Derek made his way upstairs. The bathroom door was a splintered wreck of wood panels, hanging haphazardly from the popped twisted hinges.

He ran his fingers over the door's casing. It was trashed. He was going to have to replace the entire thing.

Tomorrow.

Before he could turn away, Derek grabbed ahold of the doorframe to support himself. The empty bottle, along with what few pills remained, were strewn across the floor.

He stared down at the little white tablets, their presence accented by the black squares of the intricate pattern of black and white tiles. Every additional pill had been capable of tipping the scales from life to death. They dissolved in the toilet before he'd even flushed them away.

As if they knew they'd failed in their attempt.

Derek's heel came down with a satisfying crunch, the orange plastic of the prescription bottle shattering beneath his boot. He'd clean up the mosaic of pieces later.

He wandered down the hall to Justin's bedroom.

The shudder in his chest as he entered the room caught him by surprise. His experience in this room consisted solely of the length of time it had taken to construct it, plus the few times he'd borrowed clothes from the depths of Justin's walk-in closet.

It was a warm, comfortable space. Deep brown worn leather chairs nestled close to a rustic river rock fireplace and handcrafted log furniture, which Justin had become passionate about making. Each incredible piece created from the trees on his property.

He ran his hand along the smooth wood of a dresser near the door and breathed in the remnant scent of wood smoke. He was glad to see Justin was using the fireplace. It had been a nightmare to construct. As had so many other details Justin had insisted on.

Derek lowered himself onto the bed and reached for the messy pile of bedding balled up at the end of the bed, and smiled. Justin's bed, like his life, had been happily chaotic and carefree.

That had all changed now.

He was certain of that.

Derek kicked off his boots and stretched out on the bed, bringing the bulk of the bedding with him. He lay looking up at the ceiling and rubbed his lips with his fingers. He hadn't been able to stop himself from stroking Justin's head, holding his hand …responding to his kiss.

That kiss—

Justin had kissed him, unmistakably, and told him he was in love with him.

He turned his face into the fabric of Justin's pillow. The scent of Justin's skin had Derek gasping for breath as the full depth of the despair and regret he'd been carrying rushed to the surface, soaking the linen beneath his cheek.

He gathered the bedding close and scrubbed the tears from his face.

"I can't do this without you," he whispered into the pillow. "I need you."

Derek reached out across the bed, praying this was all a nightmare and his hand would come to rest on Justin's chest, that he would feel the escalating rhythm of Justin's heart beneath his fingertips. This time pulling Justin into his arms. Touching, tasting, caressing. Expressing his adoration and commitment to a man, if given a second chance, he would have undressed and treated with the infinite love, respect, and devotion he held for him.

A sob escaped his lips.

He wrenched a handful of the bedding from where Justin should have been and twisted it within his fist as mercilessly as the anguish dismantling him.

The Justin he knew. The one he'd fallen in love with. Might be gone.

A bang from somewhere in the house, along with his phone alerting him to a text message, startled him. He snapped his phone closed after reading the single line, "I'm here," which answered both disturbances because both were a result of Breanne making good on her threat.

She was in town, and she was downstairs.

"Fuck," Derek mumbled under his breath as he wiped the tears from his face, then he righted himself, so he was sitting on the edge of the bed. The sound of luggage dropped onto the front entry tiles confirmed her arrival.

A voice floated up from downstairs. "Hello?"

"I'm upstairs!" Derek wasn't sure he could muster the energy to stand. What he wanted to do was crawl back into Justin's bed, and sleep off the three nights he'd spent propped up in the reclining visitor's chair in Justin's hospital room.

"Derek?"

Derek sighed. "Yes!"

"Where are you?"

"Up. Stairs."

"Is Justin up there with you?"

"No," Derek answered with a diminished strength in volume that contrasted how much he wished Justin *were* there with him. It certainly would have surprised Breanne if she'd walked in on them.

"What happened to the bathroom door?" Breanne asked as she sashayed into the bedroom, discarded her sleek black clutch atop Justin's dresser, and strolled around the room, visibly unimpressed with the earthy rustic décor of Justin's bedroom.

"Accident." Derek chucked the pillow he'd been clutching back toward the top of the bed.

"Still a man of few words, I see," Breanne retorted, then made her way to stand in front of Derek, sizing him up for the first time since she'd entered the room. "You've aged."

Derek snorted out a laugh, picked up his boots, and pushed past her.

"Funny how seven years will do that," he said.

"Has it been that long?"

Derek stopped at the top of the stairs, almost gagging on the cutting words that had nearly shot from his mouth. "You know it has."

A soft, almost regretful sigh, over his left shoulder had him reconsidering his resolve to ignore her, but he headed downstairs, convinced it was the best thing. He was in no mood to re-open old wounds when there were current ones that needed his attention.

"Where's Justin?"

Derek turned to face her, eyeing her up. It didn't appear she was suspicious of anything. He stepped into the front entry and slipped his boots back on.

"Away," he answered finally.

Breanne simply nodded at him.

"Right," she said at last. "You're always so concise."

"Don't start, Bree." Derek retreated from her and scrubbed an anxious hand through his hair, his work boots beating a noisy path across the hardwood plank flooring of the kitchen. "I was checking on the place."

He flicked the lights off in the back hall, then motioned toward the front door, indicating she should head that way. He didn't care if she assumed she'd be staying here. She wouldn't be. Not on his watch. Not if he could help it. She needed to find other accommodations.

Breanne grabbed Derek's arm as he pushed past her to open the front door.

"And that required you to be on his bed?" she asked.

Derek yanked his arm from her grasp. "I was tired."

"Tired of what?" Breanne replied. "I know I'm tired of running."

Derek stopped his retreat, and his jaw clenched tight. Apparently, old wounds were going to be ripped open tonight after all. He turned to face her.

"You took off on me. You took off and left me here on my own, to deal with everything. All of it. On my own."

Breanne settled back on her heels, crossing her arms.

"I know. And I'm sorry. I never meant to hurt you."

Derek scowled and stuffed his hands deep into his pockets as if keeping them hidden from sight would somehow keep his emotions hidden. Maybe even keep the past from finding him.

"Do we have to talk about this right now?" he asked.

"No, not really."

"Thank you."

"Except, judging by the fact you're checking on *his* house …" Breanne appeared to be considering her next words, then smirked. "Oh dear. You're not together yet. That's such a shame."

"Breanne, stop. I mean it."

"Fine." She relaxed her stance. "So, have you told him yet?"

"Told him what?"

"Don't be coy." Breanne took a step toward him and placed her hands on Derek's shoulders. "You know exactly what I'm talking about."

Derek released himself from Breanne's grasp. "I said, I don't want to talk about this."

"All right—fine." She looked around the front foyer, then turned back to Derek. "So, where do you live? I tried your apartment, but apparently, you no longer live there."

"I moved."

"Yeah, I figured that out for myself." She squinted at him. "Your neighbor was extremely chatty. She told me you still own the place but that it's been empty for years."

"You know I couldn't stay there."

"So, why didn't you sell it?"

"Bree—"

"Okay, I'm sorry." Breanne tugged at the edge of her sweater while staring down at her boots. She smoothed the knitted fabric out across her hips. "Where did you move to?"

Derek scrubbed his hand around to the back of his neck.

"I bought the house next door."

"To Justin's? To this house?" She laughed out a breath. "Oh, sweetheart. What am I going to do with you?" She stepped forward, tapping a finger to Derek's chest. "So, tell me. Why isn't my brother answering his phone? And why hasn't my dad heard from him in days?"

"He's out of range. Fishing trip."

"Oh—please. Justin hates fishing."

Derek shrugged. "Okay, I don't know. He didn't tell me."

It wasn't up to him to decide how much of what had happened to Justin he wanted to share with his family. Maybe part of it. Maybe none at all. His family had been through enough after the death of his brother, Adam, three years back.

"You're keeping something from me." Breanne licked her lips and set a hand on her hip. "You get all twitchy when you're lying."

Derek reached out and grabbed Breanne's wrist, restraining her.

"Drop it. I mean it," Derek said. "You're always pushing me."

Breanne yanked her arm away. "Jeez. Chill out, would you?"

She took a step back. "I'm only here for a few days. I want to know what my little brother is up to, and how he's doing. That's it. No malicious intent."

Derek shook his head. "Nothing. He's not *up to* anything." He rubbed his temples, attempting to relieve the headache building there. "And he's fine."

He exhaled in finality and turned away. Whether Breanne was Justin's sister or not, she'd abandoned them all. She hadn't even shown up for their brother's funeral.

Justin had been inconsolable. Justin and his brother, Adam, had been close. All three of them had been close. They'd both been so incredibly proud of Adam when he'd enlisted in the military.

The least Breanne could have done was show up in support of Adam's sacrifice. He'd died overseas defending their country.

"I should head home," Derek said. "I forgot I asked your dad to drop Tucker off at my place."

Breanne extended the handle of her suitcase. "Gawd, is that old dog still around?"

Derek ushered Breanne out the front door. "More than I can say about you," he whispered to himself. "You can wait at my place until your dad shows up."

"I suppose I should tell him I'm in town ...before he gets to your place."

Derek rolled his eyes. "You haven't told them?"

He threw Breanne's luggage into the back of his truck and

held the passenger door open for her. He didn't know why he was surprised. It was such a Breanne thing to do. Leaping in and out of their lives without consideration for anyone's feelings.

That's not fair.

Not really.

"I want to be there for Dad." Breanne slammed her door as Derek slid into the driver's seat. "I thought I'd surprise him. Cheer him up a bit. He's going through a lot."

Derek had been about to start the engine—but stopped.

"What do you mean?"

"Mom. Didn't Justin tell you?"

Chapter Nine

"Wow." Breanne turned in her seat. "I can't believe Justin's been keeping this from you." She twisted a handful of her long hair within her hand, then released it. "Mom has Alzheimer's."

"What?" Derek furrowed his brow. "She seemed fine the last time I saw her."

"She must've been having a good day." She leaned her head against the headrest. "My poor dad. Mom has been leaving the house and wandering off in the middle of the night, which scares the hell out of him. He hasn't been able to sleep a full night for weeks."

Breanne took a moment before she spoke again. "She hasn't been cooperating when he asks her to bathe. When he tries to help, she starts hitting him, as if she has no idea who he is. And I think that's been the hardest on Dad. Mom not recognizing him."

Derek slumped into his seat.

He'd been wondering what was up with Justin. Now his increasingly reckless drinking, his falling behind on repairs and the existence of those pills made sense. He'd looked up Lorazepam on Justin's phone while he'd been waiting for him to come out of his coma. From what he could gather, Justin had been using the medication for anxiety and stress.

Why didn't Justin tell me about his mom?

And why didn't he tell me he was gay.

The same reason you never told Justin about Maureen.

Or your mom.

They'd both chosen to keep certain aspects of their lives separate. From day one, some of the crucial elements of truth and trust had been absent from their relationship.

Including our love for one another.

Breanne interrupted his thoughts. "Any plans to start the truck?"

"Sorry." Derek fired up the engine and drove down Justin's driveway. There was a shorter route to his house, the road linking their two properties, but he wasn't in the mood to endure Breanne hassling him about it.

Breanne reached over, scratching the scruff on his chin.

"So, when did this thing make an appearance?" She retreated when Derek batted at her hand. "You look like a lumberjack."

"So what." Derek turned into his driveway and parked off to one side so Justin's dad could park close to the house.

"No reason," Breanne answered as she leaped out of her seat onto the ground. She waited for Derek to retrieve her luggage from the back of the truck.

"Does Justin approve of it?" she asked as Derek pushed past her.

Derek dumped Breanne's luggage onto the front porch, the tallest piece falling over.

"No idea," he answered.

Breanne tipped her head to one side. "So, he's never run his fingers through it?"

Derek threw the front door open with unnecessary force, causing it to bounce back toward Breanne as she wrestled to haul her luggage inside.

He strode off toward the kitchen, ignoring her.

"I'll take that as a no," Breanne said as she slammed the door closed behind her.

She found Derek standing in front of his open fridge, staring into it as if he were expecting something to materialize. She set her hands on his shoulders, to move him aside, and pulled out the makings for a grilled cheese and pastrami sandwich.

"Sit," Breanne said, pointing to the kitchen table. "I'll make you something to eat. You look like you haven't slept or eaten properly in days."

Derek sunk into a chair, his head in one hand, and his elbow resting on the table.

Bree's right. Once I eat something, I'm going to bed.

Breanne found the cast iron frying pan, lit the gas range, and began rummaging around in search of butter. She set the assembled sandwich into the hot bubbling fat and turned to face Derek.

"Look, I'm not going to press you on where my brother is," she said. "I know how much you love him. And I also know you'd never do anything to betray him."

Breanne turned back toward the stove and flipped the sandwich over.

"If you're keeping a secret for him," she continued. "I'm going to trust it's what he wants."

"Thanks, Bree," Derek said and took the plate Breanne handed him. Her change in attitude, becoming the warm, caring Bree he'd confided in when Maureen's mental health had begun a steady decline, set him at ease. He couldn't have managed without her.

Breanne lowered herself into a chair across from Derek and reached across the table to set her hand on his. She left it there until he looked up.

"Are you okay?" she asked. "Seriously. You look like hell."

"I can't talk about it. I wish I could, but I can't."

"No, I know." Breanne removed her hand from Derek's and leaned back in her chair. "So, what story are we telling my dad about where Justin is? Because you know, he'll never believe the fishing story. Ever since you almost sank that stupid boat of yours, Justin is petrified of heading out on the water. We'll need to come up with a better excuse."

Derek smirked. "I meant fly fishing. Creekside."

"Fine." Breanne exhaled a quiet laugh. "Fly fishing it is." She patted Derek's arm as he stood to discard his empty plate. "Go lie down. I'll deal with my dad."

"Thanks," Derek said, nodding. The fatigue associated with the ongoing uncertainty and distress over the past few days had drained him.

Hopefully, by tomorrow, he'd have a clearer head to sort through what he was feeling.

The spring sun shone in through Justin's window, illuminating the bleak space, and warming his feet beneath the blankets. He wiggled his toes, and rolled onto his side, staring at the chair Derek had occupied while he'd been in a coma.

A chair that had remained conspicuously empty since then.

He brushed his lips with his fingers, remembering the feel of Derek's rough, calloused hand in his own, and the acceptance of his kiss.

Their only kiss. Never to be repeated.

Derek had made that quite clear by his absence.

He had been discarded.

His love for Derek rejected.

Justin clapped his hands over his ears.

Stay out!

Grunting. Cursing.

Get out!

Brutal hands upon his flesh.

Blackness. Panic.

Bitch.

Bitch.

Take it all, bitch.

His gut coiled.

Pain.

…so much fucking pain.

That sound—

Stop—stop—stop!

…please make him stop.

Justin rolled onto his back, staring up at the ceiling, then clenched his eyes shut, containing the latest wave of tears.

The peace and quiet was only sporadically interrupted by the sound of Karen giggling in the next tent. Subtle in comparison to the sounds they'd been subjected to earlier in the night, while Sam and Karen took advantage of the fact there were no parents around.

"Maybe they'll finally go to sleep," Derek said as he rolled to face Justin. He tugged at his sleeping bag and covered his shoulder with it.

Justin snorted out a laugh. "God, I hope so."

"Too weird, isn't it?"

"What's too weird?" Justin scratched at his nose and brushed some stray hairs from his eyes. "Sam and Karen?"

Derek was silent, his breath barely audible.

"Justin?" he whispered at last. "What happens when you have a girlfriend you want to bring camping with us? I guess I'll have to buy my own tent."

"I guess." Justin chewed at his bottom lip, and ran his tongue along both top and bottom, wetting them. "Same goes for you. If you have someone ..."

Derek's exhalation broke the silence of Justin's pause.

"Someone special, you know?" Justin continued. "I'd be all right with it, whoever it is. I promise. I'll always be your best friend."

"Justin ...," Derek whispered, then fell quiet.

Justin reached for Derek, his hand coming to rest on Derek's shoulder. "It's okay. I know. You don't have to say anything. I already know."

Derek had nodded in the dark stillness, offering a quietly spoken *thank you*. And that had been the entirety of Derek's *coming out* to him.

Their meeting had happened quite by accident. Justin wasn't an avid skateboarder, but he had headed down to the local park regardless, hoping to renew a few friendships before starting his junior year. As soon as he'd stepped up to the edge of the bowl, he'd been mesmerized by a guy at the far side. Tall, dark, and ridiculously gorgeous for a guy.

Justin had never seen him before, so he'd assumed he was new to the neighborhood. And *new guy* was taking the most ridiculous risks to gain a glimmer of acceptance from the other skateboarders, but Derek's act hadn't fooled him for a second.

He knew Derek's excessive hunger for acceptance came from somewhere much more profound. Justin knew because he'd been there. The wondering, the confusion. The denial. The desperate pleas to some unknown deity to make him *normal*.

The reality of his own sexuality had bludgeoned him earlier in the summer, making him question every friendship he'd ever had. His hunger for acceptance had consumed him after that.

He'd wanted to prove to himself that he could make and maintain friendships with guys without thinking of them in *that* way.

When Derek had headed in his direction with a smile, a nod, and an introduction, Justin knew his friendship with Derek would be different. And it had been.

They'd become inseparable, fueling Justin's hopes that someday they'd decide to take their friendship to the next level, but that day had never come.

Justin pushed his locker shut as he watched Derek work his shy-guy routine at the far end of the hallway, the accentuation of his every hushed whisper, paired with the scuffing of purportedly anxious virgin feet, a strategy that always seemed to work for him.

The guy he was speaking to, a new student, appeared to be succeeding in becoming the next contestant in Derek's never-

ending parade of high school gay-boy conquests.

"Hurry up," Justin whispered and smacked his head back against the metal locker, the sound echoing the extent of his annoyance to the far end of the hallway.

The final bell of the day had rung twenty minutes ago.

Justin groaned in despair, which thankfully crept out sounding more like irritation. Tedious and agonizing didn't adequately describe Derek's shallow crusade.

When Derek shot him a glance, Justin rolled his eyes and flipped open his chemistry textbook.

It was Friday, which meant Derek was scoping out his options for the weekend. The fact he and Derek had plans to go camping seemed to have been forgotten.

"Hey," Derek said as he nudged Justin. "Are you ready to go?"

"Seriously?" Justin pushed his backpack at Derek. "I was ready twenty minutes ago." He let go of the bag, forcing Derek to pick it up. "You can carry my backpack as thanks for me waiting."

"Yeah, whatever." Derek burst ahead of Justin, reaching the bike rack before him. "Xbox?"

Justin sighed. "Sure." He swung his leg over his bike and caught up with Derek. "So, new guy. Does he have a name?"

"Who?" Derek wrinkled his brow.

"The guy you were talking to. Does he have a name?"

"Probably." Derek shrugged. "I didn't think to ask."

Justin applied the brakes on his bike and came to a full stop.

"You didn't make plans to meet up with random no-name boy this weekend, did you? Because you and I are supposed to go camping. You promised me you wouldn't jam out on me again."

"Was that this weekend?" Derek slowed and circled back. "I'm sorry. I forgot."

"How, Derek?" Justin settled back on his seat. "No. Why? Why do you keep forgetting?" He rolled his bike forward as though he were about to take off.

"I thought you were my best friend," he added with some reluctance.

"I am." Derek came to a stop beside Justin and slid off his seat to steady himself.

He stepped closer and placed his hand on Justin's shoulder. "Justin, you're more than a best friend. You're like a brother to me. I wouldn't have it any other way. You know that."

Justin's mood shifted as the hospital room took on a different atmosphere, the sun withdrawing, removing its warmth from the space. He curled up on his side, hugging a pillow to his chest.

Like a brother.

An annoying, insignificant brother.

Only of any use when Derek wanted something.

"Jeez, Derek. What the fuck?" Justin pulled away from Derek's grasp and stormed off toward the only store open at that time of night. Cigarettes had seemed a necessity if he was going to keep himself from killing his so-called best friend.

Some beer would've been a blessing as well, but they were both underage. The fact that Derek was drunk meant he'd likely hooked up with some guy much older than himself. Again.

So there he was, three o'clock in the morning, awoken by a call from Derek, summoning him to pick him up.

"Justin ...wait." Derek stumbled after him, half running, half attempting to maintain his balance. "Justin!"

"Don't!" Justin let the door of the store close in Derek's face and hustled to reach the far end of the store before Derek could figure out how to work the door and follow him.

Within seconds, Derek caught up and careened into Justin, almost knocking him into the potato chip display.

"Fuck off!" Justin knocked Derek backward and sent him crashing onto the floor, where he came to rest on his back. "You

couldn't have waited until you were finished before calling me?"

Derek crawled toward Justin, reaching for him. "I said I was sorry. I thought we were finished. But then, you know ..."

Justin shook his head vigorously. "No. You see. I don't want to know. I have no interest in knowing who you're fucking this week. And I sure as hell don't need to walk in on it."

That had been the last time he'd subjected himself to what could be described as self-inflicted torture. Seeing Derek like that—rugged, flushed, and freshly fucked by some random guy was too painful. He'd told Derek to stop calling him.

Justin flicked at his IV tubing as he peered over at the latest volunteer who'd been placed in his room to watch over him. Pointless. He had no intention of trying to kill himself again.

At the time, ending his life had seemed the only way of escaping Derek's hold on him. If he'd never met Derek, he would've been married by now. He wouldn't have been camping. He wouldn't have found himself lying next to Derek weekend after weekend, aching to be made love to by the only person he'd ever truly loved.

He wouldn't have been seeking out the affection of another man.

He wouldn't have found himself overpowered.

He wouldn't have been assaulted.

Raped.

He wouldn't have been raped.

Justin clenched his fist and slammed it into one of his pillows.

And yet, I was stupid enough to tell Derek I was in love with him.

Justin's fist came down again, shaking the bed.

He grasped the pillow, tearing at it, and pitched it across the room. The volunteer leveled a gaze at him, then went back to reading her book, having become used to his outbursts.

He stared over at her.

He needed to get up.

Justin swung his feet around and placed them on the cold floor.

He rose to his feet, but nausea had him clutching at the bed as a pinching, gripping ache punched up through his gut, his pain medication not offering him the obliteration he craved.

A reminder of what Nick had done to him.

A reminder that Derek wanted nothing more to do with him.

His body shook, near collapsing, the latest bout of despair spilling over.

Please, no more.

The humiliation rippled through him.

Fuck you, Derek.

This is your fault.

Justin gripped the loose fabric of his gown in one hand, and headed off across the room, dragging the IV pole with him. He slammed and locked the bathroom door, ignoring the excited demand from the volunteer to leave the door open.

The IV pole rattled against the sink.

The hollow emptiness of the sound echoing in the tiny space caused him to erupt, and he began thrashing the pole around, ripping the IV from his arm. "Go to hell!"

He kicked the IV pole across the room.

"Go to fucking hell, Derek!"

As drops of blood showered the bathroom floor, Justin's fist made contact with the shiny surface of the unbreakable metallic mirror above the sink.

Of course, it didn't shatter.

And that's when he truly lost it.

Chapter Ten

Derek was sitting directly across from Sam but wasn't paying him much attention, his mind occupied by other things. He'd agreed to meet Sam for lunch weeks ago to discuss his will, but it wasn't going to be as straightforward as when he'd initially made the appointment.

So much had changed since then.

"Derek." Sam snapped his fingers.

"I don't know, Sam." Derek swilled the coffee around in his cup and tossed back the sludgy remains. It was his third successive cup. He was hoping it would help clear his head.

Sam had brought up the topic of beneficiaries, and Derek had unexpectedly found himself at a loss as to whom he should name. Last week it would have been easy. He had no living relatives other than a few third cousins, whom he'd never met, and had no idea what their names were.

He drummed his fingers on the table. There was only one person he wanted to leave everything to, but he was no longer sure where he stood with him. The kiss and Justin's declaration of love had confused things. He wasn't confident their friendship would even survive the events of the past week. The chance of a romance flourishing between them seemed unlikely.

Sam set his pen down on top of the sheet of *Parker Cole LLP* letterhead, on which he'd scribbled what few details Derek had provided him.

"Derek." He tapped the table. "Are things that bad between the two of you?"

Derek blinked, unsure if he had heard the question correctly. Sam was making some significant assumptions, implying Justin was the obvious beneficiary.

"Justin. Your best friend." Sam leaned back. "The guy you spend every waking moment with. The guy who would do anything for you."

Derek grunted out a laugh. "Are you going to start that again?"

"What." Sam shrugged his shoulders. "I'm at a loss. I truly am. You two are inseparable. And you obviously have feelings for each other."

Derek tipped his cup upside down onto the saucer and guided the porcelain around in circles a few times. He thumbed the bottom rim of the cup. The expensive restaurant Sam had picked out for them was making him uncomfortable. Not because he couldn't afford it, or that it was out of his social depth but that Sam hadn't warned him. His tattered, grubby work jeans and paint-spattered boots were attracting more than a few stares.

He decided to bite.

"What do you mean *obviously*?"

"No." Sam shook his head. "The fact you won't own up to it. I'm not going to bother. You two can work this out on your own."

Derek stroked the edge of the tablecloth, his teeth clenched to keep him from partaking in the debate Sam was *obviously* attempting to initiate.

His phone vibrated in his pocket.

"Put Justin down as the beneficiary," he said across the table to Sam as he dug his phone out. He flipped it open. It was the hospital.

"So, everything?" Sam asked.

An annoying level of uncertainty set in as Derek processed that word, *everything*. It shouldn't have. He knew what he wanted. Even if their friendship was obliterated, he wanted to leave everything he had to Justin.

His love for Justin was something he'd never abandon. Even if they never saw each other again, that love would be with him for the rest of his life.

Derek nodded yes and shushed Sam as he answered the phone call.

"Fine," Sam murmured. "Everything it is."

"Hello?" Derek spun the coffee cup around on its saucer with more vigor than before. "Yes, this is Derek." He nodded as he spoke, and looked toward the vaulted ceiling above, his heart pounding out a frantic rhythm in his chest.

"Power of attorney? Me? I don't know."

He looked at Sam, but Sam shrugged.

What the hell?

He clapped a hand over his face.

"Yes, I guess so. If that's what it says." Derek rolled his eyes. "Karen dropped it off." He peered over at Sam again, receiving another shrug. "Right, okay. Sure."

Please, tell me why you're calling.

I don't care who you are.

Just tell me.

"Is Justin all right?" Derek ran a hand into his hair, gripping and clenching the roots as he listened to the preamble of information leading up to the reason for which they were calling.

Sam leaned across the table, gesturing with his hands to know what was being said, mouthing, "Is he okay?" repeatedly.

Derek waved his hand back and forth at Sam. The persistent distraction was messing with his ability to focus on what was being said.

From what he was able to make out, Justin was okay, physically. Some significant bruising and lacerations, and a few broken bones in his hands as a result of his using the cinderblock walls of the bathroom as a punching bag.

"Yes." Derek nodded and then peered toward the front door of the restaurant. As soon as he was off this call, he was heading straight to the hospital. "Yes, I think that would be best."

He sighed, in an attempt to release the wave of sorrow

building in his gut. He brought his hand down to rest on the table. They were going to give Justin a sedative for his own safety. The damage to his physical body, diminutive in comparison to the mental turmoil darkening his mind.

"Yes, thank you."

Derek flipped his phone closed to end the call.

"Well?" Sam reached forward and grabbed Derek's arm. "What happened?"

Derek fumbled for his wallet to pitch in for his portion of the bill. "Justin flipped out. Bashed himself up pretty good." He fished around in his pocket for his keys. Upon finding them, he clamped them tight in his palm to contain them. His hands were shaking so badly, he was having difficulty keeping ahold of them. "They're going to sedate him."

"Oh, shit." Sam settled back in his chair. "I better call Karen."

"Do you mind waiting on that?" Derek scrubbed a hand across his lips, remembering the tender kiss Justin had stolen the day before. What had changed in less than twenty-four hours?

I took off on him, that's what.

"Dammit," he whispered. He knew he should have woken Justin up and said something. Told him he was coming back, but he hadn't been sure. He hadn't been sure if he was coming back. And he hadn't wanted to lie to Justin.

Apparently, abandoning him is okay though.

"Derek." Sam appeared at his side, coat in hand, waiting for Derek to tell him why he wasn't to call Karen yet.

"I need to see him first. On my own," Derek said.

Sam backed off and let Derek go without pressing him for more information. A consideration he appreciated more than Sam could know.

The nurse who'd called him had shared a small amount of detail regarding Justin's *episode as* she called it. Details he had no intention of sharing.

Hearing her recall the violent anguish she had witnessed, the anger, and rage erupting as Justin cursed his name. Screaming he wished he'd never set eyes on Derek.

It tore at his heart.

When Derek arrived at Justin's hospital room, the blinds were closed, and the privacy curtain was drawn around his bed, lights dimmed.

He nodded at the volunteer tucked into a chair close to Justin's bed, and took in the scene as he sunk into that same chair, the volunteer vacating it after communicating a silent exchange for Derek to find her when he finished his visit.

"What have you done to yourself?" Derek whispered as he reached for the swollen, split, bloodstained hand resting peacefully on the pillow beside Justin's head.

Justin's eyelids fluttered briefly, but he didn't rouse, the sedatives he'd authorized thankfully offering Justin some peace.

Derek touched Justin's cheek, brushing at the smears of dried blood in an attempt to rub them away. Even Justin's lips were coated.

He lowered his forehead to the metal bed rail.

"Go deep," Derek shouted, then threw the plastic bottle of cola, whistling with enthusiasm when Justin managed to turn around in time to catch it.

Laughing as the bubbling foam threatened to blow the cap off, Justin dropped the bottle and ran away from it, then doubled back, picked it up, and took off after Derek.

They'd both ended up a sticky mess that day. Justin had unscrewed the cap of the bottle enough to soak them both. Derek smiled into the crook of his arm. They'd skipped the remainder of school and headed to Justin's to clean themselves up. The entire bike ride to

Justin's, giggling like a couple of goofy preschoolers.

Derek brushed his thumb along Justin's lips. He'd been incredibly tempted to remove the syrupy cola from Justin's lips with his own. He'd dreamed for weeks afterward of what might have happened between them if he'd succumbed to his impulses and followed Justin into the shower.

"I'm so sorry. For everything." He lifted Justin's hand to his lips and kissed the ravaged knuckles of a hand he knew so well. "You have no idea how much you mean to me."

"What happened to you?" Derek stepped in front of Justin to block him from taking off down the street toward home. He'd waited for Justin at the bleachers for almost an hour after school. In all the time they'd been walking or riding home together, Justin had never been a no-show.

"It's nothing." Justin batted Derek's hand away and pulled up the hood of his jacket.

"Woah—hold up." Derek grabbed Justin's shoulder and hauled him off the sidewalk to a neighbor's side yard. He pressed Justin against a section of lattice and yanked the hood off Justin's head. Justin stared down at the ground, avoiding eye contact with Derek.

"Don't ...," Justin started.

"Don't what?" Derek touched his fingers to an area of Justin's cheek that was taking on a deepening purple hue. He clenched his jaw as his anger rose. "Who did this to you?"

Justin pushed Derek's hand away from his face. "I'm not telling you." He tugged the hood back into place. "I know you. You'll go after them. And this is none of your business."

Derek grunted and nudged Justin to get him moving toward home.

Justin did not need to tell him who had done this to him. He knew who it was. And it had everything to do with him.

Derek released Justin's hand back to his pillow, and dug his fingers into Justin's hair, savoring the dense feel of it, recalling every moment that he'd dreamed of doing so.

He let his fingers trail down the side of Justin's face, ending at his chin.

"I'd be so entirely lost without you."

The rings suspending the privacy curtain clattered as the curtain was pulled away, allowing the bright fluorescent lighting from the hallway to illuminate the previously intimate space.

"Mr. Lawrence?"

Derek sighed and peered up into the face of a nurse he hadn't encountered before.

"Yes."

"I spoke with you on the phone."

Justin stirred, mumbling, then quietened.

Derek lifted his hand to block the light from shining in Justin's face. "Do you mind closing that, please?"

"Sorry." The nurse flicked the curtain partially shut, then wandered to the far side of the bed, and scrolled through some readouts. "Does Justin have any other family?"

"Yeah." Derek's cheek twitched. "But I don't think he'd want them knowing he's here."

The nurse pursed her lips, then leaned over the bed, and wrinkled her nose. "We'll have someone on the night shift clean him up a bit. We're going to keep him mildly sedated for the next couple of days."

"Okay." Derek nodded, not convinced sedating Justin beyond today was the right thing to do. He had nothing against which to gauge his decision. His go-to sounding board for most of the major decisions he'd ever made in his life was lying unconscious in front of him, covered in his own blood.

Derek pulled out his phone to see what time it was. It would be hours before the night shift started. He rose to his feet, pushed past the nurse, and headed toward the linen carts in the hallway, in search of what he needed to clean Justin up.

It was the least he could do for his best friend. A guy who had suffered through more beatings in defense of his coming out than *he* ever had.

Chapter Eleven

Justin flicked the lights on behind his bed. Then off again.

Then on.

Then off.

On, off. On, off …on. A low grumble built within Justin's chest, until it erupted in a holler of frustration, followed by his pillow being chucked at the window beside the bed, rattling the nasty,   when-was-the-last-time-they-had-been-properly-cleaned, blinds.

Another roll of aggravation started to build.

He'd been there almost eight days, enduring a constant level of low physical activity. His body was accustomed to being pushed physically twelve hours a day. Often more, if he counted the hours he'd spent helping Derek with his house.

Plus, he missed his guitar.

And other things.

People. Certain people, whom he preferred not to think about anymore. It was time to move forward, not back. Time to follow his passions.

Easier said than done.

If Derek had come in and told him he was in love with him too, he might have changed his mind. No, he *would* have changed his mind. Without question. He knew that.

Now it was too late.

Derek hadn't been in to visit him.

Justin flipped open the latest magazine Karen had dropped off, in her attempt to break his life of monotony. It wasn't helping. She meant well, but he didn't want to know how to build a pergola in his backyard. Or a garden shed for that matter. He and Derek had single-handedly built entire houses together. One would hope a garden shed would be an easy task in comparison.

Derek again.

He tossed the magazine onto the pile of others collecting particulates of hospital dust.

Dammit.

Justin groaned, the boredom gnawing away at his resolve to stick this out. To stay in the hospital until his doctors cleared him to go home. The last couple of days had been moderately busy, attending support group meetings and appointments, but today, the first day of the weekend, the only busyness happening was the noise and intrusion of other patients receiving visitors.

He slid down in bed, tucked his remaining pillow behind his head, and stared up at the ceiling. Karen came to visit every day. Sometimes only for a few minutes. She had to work around a full-time work schedule and Brittany's care. She was always fun to hang with, filling him in on her daughter's latest antics and giving him reviews of the latest movies they'd watched on Netflix.

However, Sam had only stopped by once. And their exchange had been strange, halted, and unfamiliar as if they'd just recently met and had nothing in common to discuss, which was fine. He was happy Sam hadn't come back after that brief solitary visit.

In addition to the encounter being uncomfortable, he'd needed to employ some serious restraint to keep from asking Sam about Derek.

Stop thinking about him.

Justin would have sacrificed anything to erase what had happened. To erase what Derek had seen. To erase Derek altogether.

"Knock—knock." The cheery sound of Karen's voice permeated the stillness as she swept into the room, all smiles, and plopped herself down beside him on the bed.

"I have good news for you," she seemed to squeak.

Justin inhaled, holding his breath for a moment, unsure whether he should get his hopes up or not. Last time Karen had come bearing good news, it had been to tell him she and Sam had succeeded in replacing a few of the windows on the south side of their house.

He'd pretended to be thrilled with their achievement, but truthfully, their accomplishment confused him. He couldn't understand why Derek hadn't done the job for them. He was usually quick to jump in and help friends out with anything. Absolutely anything.

It doesn't matter.

"What news?" Justin asked after dismissing his concern over Derek's absence from Karen and Sam's home renovation project.

"I was speaking with one of your nurses yesterday." Karen clapped her hands together, and then placed them on Justin's cheeks. "Your doctors might let you go home tomorrow."

The shudder of dread was unexpected. Justin had been dreaming of going home, but now the impending reality scared him. He'd become accustomed to the safe space where decisions were made for him—no cooking or cleaning dishes. No laundry. No venturing out in public.

No Derek.

Justin's breath quickened. Heading home meant his chances of running into Derek increased exponentially, considering their properties backed onto one another. With summer coming, the creek, the swimming hole, the trails beyond …there was no way to know when Derek was going to be there. There was no way to avoid seeing him at some point.

"Justin?" Karen touched his arm. "Are you all right?"

Breaking from his thoughts, Justin nodded.

He slipped his arm away from Karen's grasp. "Fine," he said, and smiled as convincingly as possible, even though he knew Karen would see straight through it.

"Is this about Derek?" she asked as she slid off the bed and sat down on a nearby chair.

Justin smoothed out a ripple of sheet next to his thigh. "I have wasted far too much of my life on Derek Lawrence." He glanced up at her. "I don't want anything to do with him ever again. I don't. He's ruined every chance I've ever had of settling down."

"That's a bit harsh, isn't it? Derek sat here for the entire three days you were in a coma. He never left your damn side. As for him ruining your life, I have no idea what you're talking about. I know you want to start a family, but no one is stopping you from doing that." Karen's brow creased. "Especially Derek. He's your best friend."

Justin stared into his lap as if it contained the answer to every question he'd ever had. "You know damn well it's more complicated than that."

Karen intertwined her fingers, cupping one knee as she crossed her legs.

"Want to tell me about it?" she asked.

Tipping his head from side to side to stretch out the muscles of his neck, Justin mulled over the exact words he wanted to use.

There were only three words that adequately described how he felt.

"I love him, Karen."

"Derek."

"Yeah." Justin wrapped his arms around his waist, apprehensive about revealing a truth he'd hidden for so long. "That's why I don't want to see him."

Karen uncrossed her legs, adjusted her purse as she stood, and leaned against Justin's bed. "That makes absolutely no sense," she whispered to him. "You know that, right?"

Then she was gone, and he was left to replay the last conversation he'd ever had with Derek, in his head ...again.

"I'm right here."

And he had been. So close. So seductively close, he hadn't

been able to stop himself from kissing Derek and confessing his love for him.

"That tree there." Derek grabbed Justin's arm, hauling him off the fallen log he'd been sitting on so Justin could get a better look at an owl he said he'd spotted.

"There. See it?" Derek prompted.

"Where?" Justin crowded in next to Derek, trying to gain the same sight line as him, but he still couldn't see it. "I don't know where I'm supposed to be looking."

"There." Derek pushed the knapsack they'd brought with them out of the way, then stepped behind Justin, and placed his hands on Justin's shoulders.

"There where, Derek?"

"I'll show you."

Derek had lifted his hands to either side of Justin's face, cradling it, and guiding it.

The whisper in his ear, "See it, Justin?" accompanied by Derek's warm, gentle breath on his skin had startled him.

Justin closed his eyes, rolled onto his side, and tucked his knees up. For weeks after their hike that day, his imagination had gone wild, convinced Derek's actions had an underlying message.

His breath quickened as he returned to those few moments when their bodies had been pressed tightly against one another, their chests rising and falling in unison. The touch of Derek's hands upon his face …his chin upon his shoulder. His breath, soft as a whisper, igniting his skin. His words had seemed to mean so much more than what had been spoken.

Justin's eyes snapped open, his heart thundering.

His words had meant more.

Later that same day, after they'd found their way out of the woods, they'd been wrestling their bikes free from some brambles.

He'd repeated to Derek how he was sorry he hadn't seen the owl.

At the time, Derek's answer had seemed odd, but replaying it now, Derek's response made so much more sense.

Especially since that kiss.

Derek hadn't pulled away. He'd accepted the kiss.

No—no—no.

As Derek had ridden off that day, he'd shouted over his shoulder, "Maybe someday, you'll see it. Like, really, really see it."

Justin jammed his hands up into his hair, yanking at the roots as tears pinched his eyes, the beating of his heart whooshing and pulsing in his ears.

Derek hadn't been trying to help him spot an owl that day. There likely hadn't been an owl at all. It had been a ploy by Derek to get close to him. To press up against him, to brush his soft full lips against his cheek …to whisper his name in his ear.

Justin scrubbed his eyes with the heels of his hands. A low guttural cry of regret escaped his lips. Derek had been trying to tell him something in his stupid cryptic way that day.

He'd succeeded in convincing himself Derek wasn't interested in him.

He'd missed the true meaning of Derek's words entirely.

Chapter Twelve

Derek picked through the remaining contents of Justin's fridge, once Karen had purged it of anything expired. He was attempting to determine what most of the contents were. For a bachelor, Justin had an impressive collection of food items he'd only ever seen in the gourmet section of the grocery store. An area of the store he consciously avoided.

He moved a few things over to clear a space for the milk, bread, cheese slices, and eggs he'd picked up. Not surprisingly, filling Justin's fridge wasn't quelling the guilt chewing him up inside.

He'd tried to go back to the hospital. Made it to the parking lot a few times. Even stood outside Justin's door, staring in at him. Yesterday, he'd sat for hours in the visitors' lounge, trying to work up the courage to see him, but he hadn't been able to follow through.

Justin had poured his heart out, told him he was in love with him. Words he'd been longing to hear. And what had he done? He'd bolted like the coward he was.

Justin would never forgive him for running. And he hadn't wanted to enter his room and have Justin confirm that, to reject him once more. Except, this time, forever.

Derek dug around in a shopping bag, removing a package of bacon and some deli wrapped pastrami, and stuck them in the meat drawer.

The least he could do was make sure the guy was equipped to make some bacon and eggs and a grilled cheese sandwich when he came home from the hospital today.

He lifted what was already in the meat drawer and sniffed it.

"You have something against vegetables?" Karen asked as she peered in at what Derek had bought to restock the fridge.

"Not particularly." Derek held up the foil-wrapped mass he'd retrieved, attempting to read the mashed up label. "What is this?"

"Brie." Karen rolled her eyes at Derek's resulting blank expression. "It's a type of cheese. You bake it? Put it on crackers?"

Derek tossed it back in the drawer and closed the fridge. "Does Justin actually use all of this fancy stuff?"

Karen lowered a hand onto her hip. "Are you serious?"

Derek shrugged.

"Who do you think cooks those amazing meals he serves when we come over for dinner?" Karen asked, her fingers tapping on her hip. "Elves?"

Derek twisted the empty plastic grocery bag in his hands. "I thought he ordered in or something." He tossed the bag toward the kitchen table, but it floated onto the floor.

"Ordered in? You're telling me you've never been in the kitchen when he's cooking?" Karen held her hand to her brow. "Actually, I'm not surprised. He probably kicks you out. I know I would."

Derek looked down at the floor. They'd fallen into a habit of eating out most nights unless they were in the middle of a project, then they'd order pizza or Chinese.

"I don't know what he sees in you," she added."

"Thanks a lot, Karen."

"No, really." Karen slammed the door of the kitchen cupboard she'd been loading full of cereal, canned chili, and dried pasta. She turned to face Derek. "You know nothing about him. Justin *loves* cooking. No. He *adores* it."

She jabbed a finger in Derek's direction.

"If you hadn't coerced him into renovating houses with you, he would've gone off to culinary school, but you took that from him. Always taking. Never giving."

"That's not fair. I never coerced Justin into anything. He's a grown man. We started a business together. That's it."

"That's it, he says," Karen mimicked. "On the topic of taking and never giving. Is the elusive Breanne still in town?"

"No, she was only here for a few days."

"Figures."

"She's coming back. Moving back."

"Breanne is moving back ...here?"

"Yeah, her dad needs her help."

"Why?" Karen gathered up an array of the cardboard and plastic wrap from the packaging of the canned goods. "Or is that an excuse. Did she run out of money?"

Derek exhaled, setting his hands on his hips. "No, she needs to be here for her dad."

Karen stopped what she was doing. "Why? What's going on?"

"Justin's mom. She has Alzheimer's. Breanne is moving back to help her dad find a care facility and generally take over around the house. Her dad is feeling pretty lost."

"Shit ..." Karen reached for the counter. "I've been in there visiting Justin every day, and he never said anything to me. Did he say anything to you about his mom?"

"No. Nothing."

Karen faced the counter. "No wonder he's been acting stranger than normal. Dealing with his mom must have been draining him." She turned toward Derek. "I can't believe he didn't tell you."

"Seems our relationship isn't as close as I thought."

"Jeez, I'm sorry."

Derek grunted, not wanting to discuss it further. He checked his phone for messages. There wasn't a single one, which wasn't a surprise. His and Justin's company wasn't doing well.

He turned his attention back to the reality of picking Justin up.

I can't do it.

The rapid beating of his heart battered at his breath as he thought about seeing Justin today. Engaging in conversation with him and sitting near enough to touch him.

He couldn't do it.

He couldn't pick him up.

"Damn." Derek looked up at Karen. "I hate to do this to you, but could you pick Justin up from the hospital?"

"Why?" Karen scowled at him. "Where are you going to be?"

Derek swiped a hand across his mouth, lifting the beads of sweat forming on his upper lip. "I have some business I need to deal with."

Anything to get out of this.

"Derek, don't." Karen crossed her arms. "Don't you dare do this to him."

"Karen, I can't pick him up. I have a business to run. I have people wanting quotes on jobs. You know work has been scarce. I can't afford to slack off when the whole business I *coerced* Justin into starting up is on the verge of going under. Things are bad."

It was a lie, the inundation of texts, but it was the only excuse he could think of.

Karen released an exasperated breath, reached for Derek's arm, and settled her fingers on his wrist. "He needs you. Please don't abandon him."

"Don't." Derek pulled his arm away. "There's so much more to it than that."

He smashed his hand into the side of the fridge, jostling it.

An array of magnets and photos landed on the floor. Derek reached down and picked up one of the pictures. Christmas, three years ago. Justin was attempting an unsuccessful headlock on him, shrieking with laughter, his face covered in orange mush after he'd caught Justin off guard, and ground an entire piece of pumpkin pie in his face.

"I fucked up." Derek returned the photo to the fridge. "I

never should have let him leave our tent and head off to Nick's. I should never have suggested he go there in the first place."

He brushed his finger across the image of Justin's face, then turned and leaned his back against the fridge. "We were close that night. So damn close to surrendering to each other. So close to pushing aside all the denial that's been plaguing our relationship."

"Whoa. Backup." Karen settled back against the kitchen table. "What happened between the two of you that night?"

"I'm pretty sure we both wanted to—you know ...do stuff. And not just as buddies or anything like that." Derek drifted away from Karen, moving to an open area of the kitchen. "It would've meant so much more than that."

Karen was silent for a moment as she stared at Derek, then she gathered up the plastic shopping bags off the floor and pitched them into the garbage under the sink.

"How long have you known?" she asked.

"Known what?"

"How long have you known you were in love with Justin?"

Derek lifted his keys from his pocket then hazarded a glance up at Karen.

"Who says I'm in love with him?"

"Don't be an ass."

"Fine." He shoved the keys back in his pocket. "It's been awhile."

"Like a month ago? A year ago?"

Derek shrugged. "Years."

"Are you kidding me?" Karen slammed her hand on the counter. "How many years are we talking about here? Five? Ten?"

"No." Derek prepared himself. Karen was about to take him down, and there was nothing he could do to stop her. He hoped she wouldn't tell Sam though.

"No meaning more or less?" Karen asked.

Derek sighed and turned away from her. "More. Lots more."

"High school?"

Karen clapped a hand to her mouth when Derek didn't object. "Oh my god. All this time you've been in love with your best friend and you did absolutely nothing about it?"

"I couldn't. I wanted to tell Justin, but I couldn't risk losing him."

"So, you strung him along for all these years instead."

"I would never do that to him. I had no idea he felt the same about me."

"I have trouble believing that, but ...you know now." Karen's eyes narrowed. "And you still haven't told him you're in love with him." She fell silent, her cheeks reddening as she glared at him. "Why?" she said at last. "Why would you do that to him?"

Derek turned away from her as she took off down the back steps without a further word.

"Thanks for meeting up with me." Derek handed Justin his last stick of Juicy Fruit gum. He'd been saving it for him, tucked away in the front pocket of his jean jacket. "I appreciate it."

"No problem."

Justin folded the gum into his mouth. He balled up the wrapper and pitched it at the red painted oil-drum, chained like a criminal to the bleachers lining their school's outdoor basketball court to function as a garbage receptacle.

Derek wheeled his bike forward, bumping at the spokes of Justin's bike.

"I couldn't stay there—"

"You don't need to explain." Justin reached out, gripped Derek's shoulder, and squeezed it. "Did you want to sleep at my house? My parents won't mind."

Derek shook his head. "It's two in the morning."

Justin shrugged. "So?"

"They're going to know you snuck out." Derek hammered the front wheel of his bike against the pavement, unsure. They'd only known each other for a few months, and Justin had told him about

his parents. About how cool they were, but he didn't want Justin to end up in trouble on his behalf.

As for his own parents, they wouldn't care if he snuck out in the middle of the night. He could disappear for days, and they wouldn't notice. Maybe his mom might, if she had a moment of clarity, but the chances of her awakening from a drunken stupor were slim. Maybe even entirely unrealistic. She loved him and had done the best she could, considering the hideously abusive situation she'd found herself in with her second husband.

She was always quick to step in and redirect his stepdad's anger away from him, and onto herself. It had left him feeling guilty and powerless.

He had no idea what he could do to save her.

"Derek." Justin touched Derek's shoulder again. "They would be more upset if they knew I left you to sleep outside."

Derek nodded reluctantly and followed behind Justin as they leaped onto their bikes to cycle the short distance to Justin's house.

Derek took a moment to look around Justin's kitchen. Every detail. Wainscoting, crown molding, white cabinets with butcher-block counters, built in wine rack, all meticulously picked out by Justin. He had an eye for detail that made him instrumental in the success of their business. He didn't want to contemplate the possibility that Justin would decide to move on.

To leave him.

He brought both hands up to cover his face and sucked a breath in past them.

This was his fault.

One night.

That's all it had taken.

Their love for each other had been sullied and poisoned. In one fucking night, before they'd even had a chance to explore the nuances and rhythm of their love for one another.

Justin hung off the edge of his mattress as he threw Derek another
pillow to add to the makeshift bed they'd assembled on the floor.

"Are you sure you're okay on the floor?"

"I'll be fine." Derek hauled the thick, colorful Spider-Man
blanket up over his shoulder. He squirmed until he was somewhat
comfortable atop Justin's bedroom carpet.

"If you change your mind ...," Justin offered as he touched
Derek's shoulder. He drew his arm away and switched off the light
situated on his bedside table. "There's lots of room up here."

Derek almost groaned aloud. Watching Justin undress for
bed had nearly done him in. Climbing into bed with him was the
last thing he wanted to do. Justin's caring nature, his smile, his
eyes, his humor ...his body. He wasn't sure he would've been able
to stop himself.

Then what? If he whispered the things he'd dreamed of
saying, Justin would never speak to him again, and everyone in
school would find out he was a dirty little faggot.

Derek slammed Justin's kitchen door behind him and took off for
his truck. He shouted at Tucker to hurry up and jump into the cab,
but Justin's black Labrador Retriever ignored him. The old dog
had recently decided it was his right to take as long as he wanted,
now that he was a senior.

Once in the cab, he ruffled the fur on Tucker's shoulder as
the dog curled up against his side. Taking care of him had been
difficult. He was a constant reminder that Justin was the one
paying the price for their denial. Tucker nudged Derek's thigh,
then licked the seam of his jeans.

Derek pushed his nose away. It had also been therapeutic
having him around the house. The curious dog, now gnawing at a
rawhide bone, knew him as well as he knew Justin. They'd both
cared for him from the day he was a puppy.

Tucker used to come everywhere with them, including
camping when he was younger. Now there was too much worry

he'd wander off, so they'd started leaving him behind.

Derek took off for home, opening up the massive engine to take advantage of the straight road they'd cleared between their two properties. He didn't slow down until the long gravel road connecting Justin's home to his, emptied onto his own driveway.

He pounded the brake and drifted to a stop, spraying gravel onto the cement pavers leading to his house. Pavers Justin had insisted they set in a brick-lined herringbone pattern.

The engine died as he removed the keys.

Derek sat in the stillness, his hand atop Tucker's head. The house he'd bought was nestled further into the trees than Justin's, fulfilling a deliberate attempt to live somewhere shielded from the chaos of everyday society. He'd survived enough chaos growing up in a violent alcoholic home. All he wanted now was peace.

And Justin.

He slammed his hands against the steering wheel, threw his truck door open, and wandered off down one of the many paths leading to the far end of his property.

Tucker followed along at a leisurely pace, his nose keeping him busy. There was little chance he'd become lost in these woods surrounding his home.

Golden light filtered through the canopy of massive trees and pooled in shifting puddles on the moss-veiled forest floor. Derek's body relaxed as the sounds and smells of the forest enveloped him. He slipped into the hammock he'd strung up between two giant spruce trees last summer. Of course, Justin had helped him.

Everywhere he turned was something Justin had touched.

"Are you sure?" Justin asked as he wandered through a kitchen that had been stripped bare. Fridge, stove, and dishwasher. Gone. Countertops. Gone. Sink and faucet. Gone. All that was left were some battered oak veneer cabinets. And they were utterly unsalvageable.

The rest of the house wasn't much better. It had been foreclosed on, and the owners had decided to strip the entire house bare. There wasn't a single light fixture left, and many of the walls were peppered with an assortment of holes in varying sizes.

"It's exactly what I'm looking for," Derek replied, his mind racing with ideas for bringing the house back to life.

"Derek, we have our plate full with paying jobs." Justin picked at a piece of peeling wallpaper. "We don't have time to take this on." He kicked at one of the broken chunks of drywall that littered much of the floor. "Are you sure you want to do this?"

"Absolutely." Derek paced off toward what might have been the dining room. "I love a challenge. Plus this house makes us neighbors."

Justin sighed. "True." He leaned back and propped himself back against the bare edge of the counter-less cabinet as Derek approached.

"Come on, Justin. It'll be fun."

He could've bought the house regardless, but he'd wanted Justin to be on board. He'd wanted a reason for Justin to continue hanging with him after their business day had ended.

A cold wind blew across him, reminding him it was still early in the year. Derek grunted, rolled himself out of the hammock, and headed for the house. He let himself in through the back door, headed for the living room, and took up a new place of repose on the sofa.

Before Derek had a chance to stuff a pillow behind his head, Tucker licked his face, then curled up near the front window, where he'd stationed himself on sentry duty.

Derek rubbed his hand across his eyes. Finding ways to be in Justin's company had become an obsession. Ever since that first night when Justin had invited him to sleep over. The night he'd needed to escape the sounds of his mother taking another beating.

He hadn't realized his feelings for Justin weren't strictly feelings of friendship until that night.

That his feelings for *any* guy could be so strong.

That he truly was gay.

Derek relaxed and let the memory of that night guide him. He hadn't been able to sleep, instead listening to Justin breathing from the bed above him. There had been a few times when he'd almost abandoned all reason and climbed up there with him.

The image of Justin rolling over to face him, stripping his shirt off over his head, so he could taste and tease Justin's skin with his lips, had tempted him.

He ran a hand across his chest. The image of Justin sighing as he freed himself so that he could take the full length of Justin's cock into his mouth.

Justin's body bucking, his breath quickening.

Moaning.

Justin biting at his flesh as he filled him with his cock.

Derek brushed a hand down the front of his jeans and cupped the beginnings of arousal pressing against his zipper. He would've let Justin fuck him without a moment of hesitation.

He pressed harder, stroking the still thickening girth through his jeans until intense need rippled through him. He freed the button, undid the zipper, and released his cock.

He shimmied his jeans and underwear off his hips and brushed his palm along the velvety soft skin. He closed his eyes, lying bare and exposed on the sofa he and Justin had shared many times over the years. He let his hands fall to his sides.

This is so wrong.

He shouldn't be using his memories of Justin for this.

Not now.

Not ever.

Derek pinched the bridge of his nose to stop the tears, but the body-wracking sobs were unstoppable. Wave after wave, an eruption of scrambled thoughts roared at him from their past.

Ever since he'd met Justin, he'd loved being in his company because of Justin's optimistic, full of life, exuberant about everything, innocent approach to living. It was the loss of that innocence destroying his image of the man he thought he knew.

Not only because of what had happened to Justin but also because of the life Justin had been leading in secret.

Derek covered his face, attempting to steady his gut-churning reaction to the thought of Justin with another man. Kissing and caressing, tasting each other's skin, groaning, sweating, fucking ...climaxing—

Bile rose in his throat.

Fuck.

Chapter Thirteen

Derek switched off the radio with some reluctance as he pulled into the hospital parking lot and found a spot, interrupting an acoustic rendition of a song in Justin's permanent repertoire.

Typically, he didn't listen to stations that played the folksier tunes, but he'd been unable to quiet the looping repetition of those same songs in his head. Songs Justin had sung on a regular basis while they were working together.

Songs he found himself desperately needing to hear.

"Justin!" Derek shouted, and laughed. "Buddy, you're killing me. You've been on that same song all morning."

"Practicing," Justin shouted back.

They were working on a three-story house, replacing the flooring. The current lack of carpeting and the openness of the house meant Justin's voice was echoing throughout the entire space.

"Practicing for what?"

A loud thump, followed by a burst of cursing was the only response.

Then there was silence.

"What'd you do?" Derek set his nailer down and rose to his feet. "Justin?"

"I'm all right." Justin strode into the living room, approaching Derek after thundering down the stairs from the bedrooms. "Caught my thumb on the edge of the jamb-saw. Fucking hurts is all."

"Let me look," Derek said and grabbed for Justin's hand, a hand that was dispensing a trail of bloody droplets onto the

subfloor.

Justin was right. It didn't look too bad.

Derek touched his hand, recalling the warmth of Justin's in his own on the job site that day. And during the countless hours in Justin's hospital room.

"Give it to me!" Derek leaped at Justin, who was attempting to abscond with the latest set of plans for the reconfiguration of his new house, the one he'd convinced Justin to help him renovate.

Now, they were having fun with it—the entire project starting as a blank slate they had complete control over. No clients to deal with. Only their own ideas.

And Justin had plenty of ideas.

"Justin, cut it out. Show them to me."

"I barely changed anything, I promise." Justin surged forward, jousting Derek with the roll of plans, then knocked Derek on the head with them and took off down the back hallway to outside.

Derek jogged after him, knowing Justin would be headed straight for the creek that ran along the backside of both his and Justin's properties. They'd built a woodshed slash "get away from the world" space, including an expanse of decking large enough for a couple of chairs.

As predicted, Justin was stretched out in one of the cloth, sling-type chairs they'd deemed too far-gone to take with them camping. Here though, out in the woods behind the house, only the two of them, they got a kick out of the balancing act required to keep themselves from falling through the torn fabric onto the decking.

The new house plans were perched beside Derek's assigned chair. He set them aside and popped open the cooler they'd stocked earlier.

"Beer?" Derek asked. A quick snort from Justin meant he needn't have bothered asking. He tossed one in Justin's direction.

"So," Justin started. "Hope you don't mind, but I moved the kitchen." He cracked open his beer and poured the contents in their entirety down his throat, languishing for effect, then he crushed the can and tossed it into the allotted bin behind them.

"Yup," he continued. "Moved it upstairs to where the master bedroom was. And moved the master bedroom into the attached walk-in closet. It'll be a tight fit, but it'll be cozy, and if you're hungry during the night ...voila, the kitchen is right there."

A nearly imperceptible laugh rumbled from Derek's chest. "Ha-ha. You're freakin' hilarious, Leary." He tapped on the armrest, wrinkled his brow, and turned to face Justin.

"How's your hand," he asked, indicating Justin show him.

"It's fine." Justin rubbed his gritty thumb over the healing wound, tearing it open. "Okay, so it was fine. Now it's not. Thanks a lot for making me touch it."

Derek laughed for real this time, shoving Justin in the shoulder.

"Jeez, you're an idiot."

The truth was he'd been fishing for a reason to have Justin place his hand in his again. The feel of his buddy's rough, rugged hand in his own had rattled the lid of a deeply buried box of emotions from the past. Feelings he'd been struggling to restrain of late.

Derek released a sigh, leaped from his truck, and headed for Justin's ward. Karen had outright refused to pick Justin up, leaving him no choice. He had no idea what to expect.

He nodded at the unit clerk on his way past the nurses' station. She'd been incredibly sweet to him when he'd been waiting for Justin to wake up, bringing him coffee and sandwiches.

During those three days waiting, he'd had difficulty

relinquishing his hold on Justin's hand. The warmth of it in his own was the only intimate skin on skin contact he'd ever shared with him.

More than once, he'd nodded off, his face balancing on the metal guardrail of Justin's bed, his hand still clutched tight to Justin's. He'd gone from that level of intense support, refusing to leave Justin's side, to jamming out and leaving Justin to fend for himself. Too scared to support Justin once he woke up, in case he wanted to talk about what had transpired with Nick.

It would have been impossible for him to remain in the room if Justin began speaking about that night. He'd been struggling to suppress what he'd seen. What he knew had happened between Justin and Nick. Nick's hot breath, his mouth, his hands, his cock, all violating Justin's body.

He'd witnessed it all.

It was an image that hurled bile up into his throat.

Karen had tried to pick up where he'd left off, but with a full-time job and the demands of family life, she'd spent more time bitching at him to visit Justin than sitting with him herself.

Derek peered through the tiny window of the door into Justin's room. He pressed his forehead against it, watching Justin pack up the few things Karen had brought in for him.

The angle of Justin's shoulders as he reached for things, the curve of his back as he pressed the clothes into his bag, the way he shifted from foot to foot …the movement of Justin's body was so familiar to him. He hadn't realized how much attention he'd been paying to it over the years.

He ground his head against the window, steadying his breath. The temptation to run into that room, slam Justin up against the first flat surface he could find, and smother Justin's mouth with his own, surrendering to the love he'd been guarding, was daring him to act.

Derek cleared his throat and pushed the door open.

"Hey," he said. "Are you ready to go?"

"What the fuck are you doing here?" Justin spun around to face Derek and pitched his bag at the floor. "I told Karen to keep you the fuck away from me."

Great.

Thanks a lot, Karen.

"She didn't say anything to me."

Justin picked his bag up off the floor and threw it onto the bed. "There is no fucking way I'm getting a ride with you."

"Fine!" Derek's stomach clenched. "Walk home!" He turned toward the door and yanked it open, ready to storm out. "See if I care," he shouted over his shoulder.

"That's just it," Justin yelled. "I don't think you do care."

Derek stopped his retreat. "Don't you dare say that to me." He turned back toward Justin and strode across the room straight at him. "When it comes to you, I care plenty, so don't ..." He reached up, gripped Justin's face, and brushed a thick thumb across Justin's cheek, his body aching to kiss him. "I thought I'd lost you. I would've given anything to get you back."

For a moment, Justin remained still.

"Too little, too late." He swatted Derek's hand away. "It's been over a week. If you had any feelings for me, you should've said something by now. Now fuck off and leave me alone."

"Justin, come on, I—"

"No, I mean it. We're done. I wish I'd never met you."

Derek stumbled back as if he'd been punched in the chest.

"Justin, please ..."

"Don't," Justin said and stalked off toward the far side of the room. "I can't do this with you anymore." He leaned against the wall, his arms crossed as he stared at Derek.

"Do what?" Derek asked.

"This." Justin motioned back and forth between them. "This co-dependent bullshit."

"Is that the way you see it?"

"From my end, yeah." Justin yanked his coat out from the

locker behind him. "We've rarely left each other's side since we met. Neither of us has any idea how to function without the other."

Derek curled his hands into fists as he took a step toward Justin. It was unusual for him to raise his voice, but he was at a loss as to what Justin was on about. And it was trying his patience.

"What the hell are you talking about?" he shouted.

"From the very beginning, we've been completely dishonest with each other about our feelings, and yet we felt the need to keep chasing each other around regardless."

"No one has been chasing anyone," Derek replied. "We're best friends."

"Are we? Best friends?" Justin tossed his coat toward the bed. It slipped off, the black leather pooling on the floor at his feet. "Do you have any idea what it was like for me, being in this room, day after day, night after night, without my so-called best friend coming to see me?"

"Justin, I'm sorry." Derek took a few tentative steps toward Justin, but Justin held out his hand. Derek stopped where he was. "You threw me off." He moved to reach for Justin but stuffed his hands in his pockets instead. "When you kissed me …and that other stuff."

Justin coughed out a laugh. "That *other stuff*? You mean when I told you I was in love with you? That *other stuff*?" He ran his hands up through his hair, leaving his fingers laced atop his head. "I should have known better. You only ever have one thing on your mind."

"I don't know what you're talking about."

"Don't play innocent. After what Sam said around the campfire, you figured out I was vulnerable. You saw the way I was looking at you. The way I've always looked at you, but you'd never noticed before."

Justin let his hands fall to his sides. "You know what I think? I think you were prepared to fuck me that night—but not tell me how you felt about me."

"I wouldn't do that to you."

"Wouldn't do what? Fuck me? Or tell me how you feel about me?"

Derek clenched his teeth as he fought to stave off the impulse to beat the crap out of Justin. Justin was goading him, but he didn't know what to say to stop him.

"Did you want into my sleeping bag that night, Derek? Did you want to slick me up? Fuck my ass? Because it wouldn't have been a big deal. It's not like I've never been fucked before. Did you think Nick was the first guy to claim my ass? The first one to drive his cock into me?"

"God, Justin." Derek clutched his stomach and turned toward the door, not wanting to see the familiar features of Justin's face screwed up into something ugly. "Stop. Please."

"Funny. That's exactly what I kept whimpering when Nick was raping me."

Derek reached for the wall to steady himself.

"Why are you doing this?"

"Doing what? Filling you in on the details of what happened because we refused to be honest with each other?" Justin slammed his fist into the metal locker behind him. "Derek! Look at me!"

"Fuck, Justin." Derek spun to face him. "What do you want me to say?"

"Nothing. Absolutely nothing." Justin slipped his coat on. "We're done, you and I."

Derek placed his hand on the door and opened it, then looked back. The light above the hospital bed was creating a warm glow behind Justin's head, illuminating his scrappy blond hair.

He gripped tight to the handle. Even with his face flushed, twisted by anger and hostility, Justin made his heart ache. The love he had for the man standing before him was absolute. An emotion he would never have a chance to share with him.

Not now.

Not after everything that had happened.

He needed to back away ...for good.

"I'll call you a cab," he said.

Justin nodded. "Thank you."

And that was that.

Derek stormed out of the room and buried his feelings, thankful he'd dropped Tucker off at Justin's house earlier in the day.

Chapter Fourteen

Justin lifted the squared off loaf, of what was advertised on the packaging as white bread, from the fridge. The thin foil wrapper crinkled as he squeezed what he assumed would be an enduringly fresh feeling baked good.

He tossed it into the trash and peered back in the fridge.

What the fuck is all this stuff?

He turned the non-organic, non-free-range eggs to face him, and lifted them to check the expiration date. Worst-case scenario, he might be able to use them in a potato salad.

He set them back and opened the meat drawer.

Cheddar, bacon, and pastrami.

He closed his eyes.

Derek.

He slid both vegetable crisper drawers open.

They were both empty.

Definitely Derek.

Tucker pushed in beside him and leaned against his shoulder, suggesting a snack was required.

Justin tore open the butcher paper and handed him a piece of pastrami. At least Derek hadn't picked something as noxious as bologna.

Maybe he'd been too hard on Derek, but if the guy refused to fess up about his feelings, there wasn't much he could do about it. He was tired of playing games with him.

Either Derek loved him, or he didn't.

Except he knew damn well Derek did.

After clearing his thoughts, Justin gathered up the remaining section of Brie and a glass container of his homemade, red pepper jelly and went looking for some whole-wheat crackers.

He set everything on the counter, and went to recheck both the front and back door to make sure they were locked, then threw himself on the sofa, and flicked on the television.

He settled on the *Home and Garden* channel. His favorite contractor was ripping apart the shoddy construction completed by another builder.

Justin grinned in agreement. The wood stove hadn't been installed correctly. He and Derek had made a similar discovery in the last house they'd renovated. The occupants were lucky the fireplace hadn't started a fire in their walls.

He lay his head back against the sofa cushion, staring up at the ceiling. They'd received an award from the city's historical society for that renovation. When the City had called to inform them, Derek had been so excited he'd hugged him, clinging to Justin for much longer than necessary. And the look in Derek's eyes when he'd released him had been so close to what Justin had been waiting for. What he'd been longing for.

Then it was over.

Derek had pulled away, laughing and talking, headed for the kitchen to snag another beer.

Now he knew the truth. There had been intense love radiating from those warm, seductive eyes after all.

Justin pounded his fist into the nearest cushion, then tossed his empty plate onto the coffee table, and curled up. There had been so many occasions over the years when he'd almost told Derek how he felt about him. How much he loved him.

Day after day, year after year, the timing had never been right. And he'd been certain Derek wouldn't be interested anyway. His quest for meaningless sex hadn't abated since high school, so he'd assumed Derek was happy living his life that way.

He'd been wrong.

And now it was too late.

The pamphlet for the suicide recovery center was still sitting where he'd thrown it on the footstool. He stretched and lifted the pamphlet, then flipped it open to scan the information.

He wasn't sure if he was going to bother going to the suicide support group. At the time, it had seemed the only way to stop the pain tearing at his heart. Now, he realized Derek, or anyone else wasn't worth sacrificing his life for. Including Nick, who had taken so much from him.

A smaller sheet of paper fell out from between the folds of the pamphlet. It was the address and hours of operation for the nearest HIV clinic. He would need to be tested again in a few weeks. He crumpled up the paper and chucked it at the floor, clenching his eyes shut. He'd been trying to block it out, the sound of Nick grunting and swearing as he tore into his ass.

The printed material strewn atop his footstool had brought it all back.

Justin's stomach rolled, and he leaped up attempting to make a run for the bathroom but only made it halfway up the stairs, before the contents of his stomach erupted onto them.

The red pepper jelly dripped off the front edge of the cream-colored tiles.

Red, soiled. Tainted, slipping, oozing. Blood.

Shut up, bitch.

He vomited again.

Derek slid further down in his seat, out of view, and adjusted his ball cap to shield his face. It was always a toss-up as to whether or not Justin would recognize Karen's car in the various medical center's parking lots. He owed Karen some serious favors, but Justin would have spotted his massive pickup truck with their company logo on it within seconds.

He'd tried to stay away, but the emotion in Justin's eyes before he'd erupted, spewing hateful words at him, had exuded confirmation. Justin's love for him was as intense as his own.

And it had been haunting him.

He dismissed the memory and struggled to stretch his legs out. The *compact* car continued to cause his tall, muscular frame an immense amount of grief.

He flipped open the printed sheet of paper he kept stuffed in his wallet, perusing the details of a document he could recite in his sleep. He traced his finger down the list of appointments.

Today was Tuesday. He tapped the little square containing today's appointment details. It had been five months since Justin had been released from the hospital. Five long agonizing months without Justin in his life. Karen had recommended he give Justin some time to heal, and he'd decided to take her advice. He didn't agree with her entirely. He'd rather be supporting Justin through this, but she had some valid points. The most valid being that Justin hated him right now.

Recently though, Justin seemed to be improving, his step becoming lighter each day. At first, he had only been attending outpatient sessions at the Sexual Assault Support Center, but in the past few weeks, he'd begun showing up for his scheduled appointments with the clinical psychologist his doctor had referred him to as well.

Derek squirmed in his seat. This particular psychologist specialized in incidences of male on male sexual assault. The attending physician at the hospital had told him, given time, Justin would hopefully become comfortable letting him touch him again.

Everyone at the hospital had assumed he was Justin's boyfriend because instead of anyone in his immediate family, Justin had listed him as his next of kin on every medical and insurance document that required him to specify one.

Plus, some of the nurses had seen Justin kiss him.

Derek groaned.

That kiss.

It had taken him by surprise. Sure, he'd been thinking about doing the same, but Justin had beat him to it.

No, he didn't.

I chickened out because I'm an idiot.

Hence the stalking.

He kicked the brake pedal, knocking a clump of construction mud onto the already sullied carpeting. Karen was going to kill him if he didn't vacuum her car today.

He'd forgotten to stop at a service station to clean the interior yesterday and had been subjected to her wrath.

Derek checked the time, closed his eyes, and set his head against the headrest. There wouldn't be enough time to make it to the job site again today. He'd already delayed the start date of this particular renovation job for as long as he could without losing the contract.

It didn't matter though. The company was spiraling with or without another paltry contract. His accountant had run out of ideas to keep them from having to file for bankruptcy. No one was investing in renovations or new builds. If the business had any chance of surviving this downturn, he needed to sell his apartment. It had been sitting empty for years anyway. As soon as they'd installed appliances and replaced the lights in the house he'd bought next door to Justin's, he'd cleared the apartment out. Sleeping in an unfinished house was preferable to going home every night to that haunted, empty space.

He pinched the bridge of his nose as he tucked his head against his chest. He didn't want to go back to that apartment. Ever. Which was unrealistic. He'd have to collect the few things he'd left behind before he sold it, but the thought of walking into that apartment again terrified him.

Derek stared out the window. He hated following Justin around, but he'd decided to respect Justin's wishes by staying out of his life. Visibly anyway. The thought of being completely removed, never seeing Justin again, he wasn't ready to take that step.

He couldn't take that step.

He visualized what might have been. What still might be. He wasn't willing to accept it was over between them, even though he'd told Sam to proceed with the process of dividing their company as Justin's lawyer had requested. It was for the best. The price his realtor assured him he'd walk away with after selling the apartment would cover the debts owed by *Lawrence & Leary Custom Homes & Renovation*, and keep them from having to file for bankruptcy. There would even be enough money left for Justin to bank. He personally didn't want a single penny of it.

The sound of someone slamming a car door startled him. For a moment he panicked, worried he'd missed Justin leaving the building. He released an anxious breath, relaxing.

The timing had been perfect.

Justin climbed into his car but didn't start it. Instead, Justin slumped forward, his forehead resting on his steering wheel, his body shaking. Sobbing.

Derek gripped the door handle prepared to jump out of the car.

Don't do it.

He shifted in his seat, leaned forward, and then back again, his foot tapping on the floor.

Fuck this.

He threw his door open and bolted across the parking lot toward Justin. He was done playing games. Justin had been right. This fear and denial bullshit needed to stop.

Derek was about to knock on the driver's side window when Justin fired up the engine and turned his head to back out. He immediately caught sight of Derek pressed against the next car over. There was a moment of indecision before Justin shut the car off and rolled his window down.

"What are you doing here?" Justin asked.

"I was picking something up."

"Like what?" Justin tucked his arms across his chest. "Your latest conquest?"

"Justin—"

"What? Have I misjudged you somehow?"

"That's not why I'm here."

"Then why are you?" Justin twisted in his seat, scanning the parking lot. "And where the fuck is your truck?"

Derek squatted down to be eye level with Justin. "Look. I'm worried about you is all. I wanted to make sure you were making it to your appointments."

"You've been following me?"

"No." Derek moved his hand around to the back of his neck. His muscles were tensing. "I mean, yes. The doctor at the hospital gave me a schedule of your psychologist appointments and the times of your support group meetings. He thought I might be driving you to them."

Justin clenched his jaw. "And why would he think that?"

Derek picked at the flaking paint on Justin's door panel, fixating on it. "Because he thought we were together—a couple."

"And you didn't think to correct him?"

"No." Derek abandoned the paint and sat on the pavement. He leaned his shoulder against the door of Justin's car and looked off into the shrubbery overhanging Justin's front bumper.

Justin stared out through his front windshield. "Why not?"

Derek tilted his head and knocked it against the car door a few times. "I don't know."

"For fuck's sake." Justin undid his seatbelt and unlocked his door. "Move over." He waited for Derek to shove over, then climbed out of his car, and slid down to sit on the pavement beside him. "Why are you really here?"

Derek pitched a stone at the curb of the parking lot. "My mind keeps replaying that night. I feel guilty about what happened. You should never have been in that tent."

"But I was." Justin rubbed his nose. "During my support group meetings, I worked through the events of that night, and who I had placed the blame on. I put all of the blame on having met you in the first place. That if I hadn't, I wouldn't have been in that tent with Nick."

"You wouldn't have been." Derek tried to remain as detached as possible from the memory of that night. Even recalling the smell within the tent nauseated him.

"Maybe, but I have no regrets about meeting you. I wish our relationship had turned out differently though." Justin set his head back against the door of his car, smiling. "Every time we went camping, I'd lie there hoping you'd climb into my sleeping bag with me."

"I wish I had." Derek leaned against Justin's shoulder, basking in the closeness between them. He flicked at some chunks of drywall compound on his pant leg.

"Justin …" He knew he had no right to ask, but he needed to know. "Have there been a lot of guys?" He focused on a crack in the concrete barrier, willing his mind to cease the kaleidoscope of images containing Justin and a barrage of lovers from continuing.

Justin pulled his knees up and rested his arms on them.

"A few," he answered. "Nothing serious."

Derek nodded. "And the women you've been dating all of these years? Are you …?"

"Bisexual, yeah."

"How long have you known?"

"Long before you came to terms with being gay." Justin scrubbed his eye with the back of his hand, and then rose to his feet. "I need to go. I have an appointment at the trade school."

"For cooking, right?"

Justin leaned against his car, and his eyebrows rose as he grinned.

"Yeah," he replied. "I didn't know you knew. It's something I've always wanted to do. The fall semester starts tomorrow."

"Karen told me. And I'm happy for you." Derek dusted his hands off on his jeans and stood. "I was wondering …if you're free this weekend, could you help me dismantle that insanely dangerous deck off my kitchen?"

Justin tapped the roof of his car. "Derek, we can't go back to the way we were. I don't blame you for what happened, but things have changed between us."

A lump lodged in the back of Derek's throat as his eyes began to sting. He swiped his thumb beneath each eye, in turn, to wipe some tears away. "Am I going to see you around at least?"

He peered up at Justin in time to witness a wash of pain distort his face.

Justin, please don't do this.

"We have the same friends," Justin replied. "I'm sure we'll run into each other." He slid into his seat, closed the door, and started the car. "Derek, I'm sorry things have to end like this between us, but I need to do this for myself. I need to learn how to function on my own."

He put the car in gear, ready to back out of the spot.

"Justin wait ...please."

Derek gripped the edge of the window frame and looked down at the ground.

Justin sighed. "Please what?"

"I need to know if you're still in love with me."

Derek looked up, expecting Justin to cave and reach out for him. Drag him in for a kiss. He was not expecting to hit the ground, blood gushing down the front of his shirt, his hand cupping what was likely a broken nose.

He picked up his feet as Justin peeled out of the stall and sped off.

Chapter Fifteen

Justin paged through the trade school catalog, and then chucked it at the table. The counselor was running behind schedule, and he was becoming annoyed. He wasn't able to stop replaying Derek's question over in his mind. He needed something to distract him.

"How did your opponent fare?"

Justin looked up.

"What? I'm sorry?" he asked, searching the smiling face beaming down at him for clarification.

"Forgive me. My name is Kadema."

Kadema extended his hand and shook Justin's. "I was noticing your hand." He chuckled, pointing to it. "I cannot imagine your opponent survived a blow from a mighty fist such as this."

"No, he's fine. Trust me. He's survived worse."

Kadema covered his mouth, chuckling again. "I'm sorry. My wife says I talk too much." He waggled his finger in Justin's direction. "She also told me I must make my own friends in our new home because I am on the verge of driving her crazy."

He clapped his hands together.

Justin couldn't help but smile. The positive vibe emanating from Kadema was infectious. "My name's Justin," he said. "Are you from Jamaica?"

"Fresh off the boat." Kadema laughed. "I mean fresh off the plane. My wife, she is training to become a nurse." He patted his chest. "I came along for the ride."

"Are you planning to take some classes?"

"Yes. I am going to be a chef." Kadema grinned, an expanse of white teeth gracing the room. "Or at least a cook that can keep my wife happy. She is going to be working hard as a nurse."

Justin nodded. His mom had been a nurse. He knew all too well the number of hours required. Those days were distant memories now. She was being cared for by some of the same nurses she'd been in charge of for all those years since he was a kid.

"I've registered for the culinary certificate as well," Justin said. "I'm only here to sign some papers. Pay some money. Stuff like that."

"That shouldn't take too long."

Justin looked toward the door of the counselor's office. "I hope not. I've been sitting here for a while now."

"Maybe when you are done, we can go and drink together. My wife would be pleased."

Justin laughed. "Then I guess we better."

"Good." Kadema clapped his hand into Justin's. "We are going to be good friends, you and I. You will see."

Justin drained the remaining beer from what he estimated was his seventh, maybe eighth pint. He wasn't sure. He and Kadema had been at the *Lion's Crown* pub for hours, and they hadn't stopped talking for most of it. Kadema's enthusiasm for life was gradually pulling him out of the funk he'd been drifting around in since being released from the hospital.

As it turned out, Kadema had done a bit of construction work back home, and they were enjoying comparing notes on building techniques between the two countries. The server dropped off the latest round of drinks as Kadema leaned on the table.

"So, tell me about this fight of yours," he said to Justin. "You do not seem like a violent man."

Justin shook his head. "I'm not. Not normally anyway." He traced a finger along the edge of his pint glass. "It was my business partner." He tapped the glass. "My *ex*-business partner."

"The man you were doing the construction work with."

"Yes, but we're going our separate ways now."

"After you hit him, I should say so."

Justin snorted out a laugh. "He deserved it."

Kadema leaned back in his chair. "And what did this man do to deserve a punch from this fist of yours if you are not a violent man?"

Justin shifted in his seat. He'd promised himself that since his current friends knew he was queer, he wasn't going to hide it from any new people he met. The plan was sound in theory, but following through and being *out* to people was going to prove challenging.

"Justin?"

"He asked me if I was still in love with him." Justin looked up.

There, I said it.

"Why would he ask such a thing?"

Justin lowered his gaze and chastised himself for being such a coward. He set his shoulders and raised his eyes, meeting Kadema's straight on. "Because I am."

"In love with him? But he is a man."

Justin grinned. "Yes, I am well aware of that."

"You are a gay man?"

"Sort of." Justin watched the series of expressions erupt and then fade from Kadema's face.

"I have never known a gay man before," Kadema said finally.

"I'm sure you have. You just didn't realize it."

"That may be true. One doesn't admit to such things in Jamaica." Kadema shook his head. "No. Very unwise. Very unwise and very dangerous." He lifted his glass to his lips, and then set it back down. "So, why did you hit him, this man you love?"

"Because he's an idiot," Justin replied. "He refuses to admit he's in love with me too."

"And that is why you hit him. The man you love comes to his senses and wishes to speak with you about these feelings of love, and you hit him."

"Exactly." Justin drained his beer and slammed the glass down.

"Remind me never to tangle with a gay man," Kadema said. "If my wife hit me every time I did or said the wrong thing, I'd be covered in bruises."

Derek peered out his sliding glass door toward the back yard. The motion-sensor light had come on, illuminating the lawn down to where the dense forest began.

He laughed to himself as Tucker's face poked out from behind some brambles, startled by the bright light. The dog was always setting out on adventures in the woods he knew so well. Derek was sure it was too late for Tucker to be out wandering though.

He checked the time.

Yeah.

Eleven was too late for the aging dog to be outside on his own. It was unusual for Justin to leave him out once it was dark. There'd been some cougar sightings recently.

He stepped out onto his deck and whistled. Tucker came running and circled Derek a few times before settling down.

"Look at you." Derek rubbed his messy, twig-entangled fur. "What have you been up to out there? And where's your dad?" He pulled the most accessible bits of bramble from around Tucker's eyes, and then held his face, smoothing his fur. "Let's find out, hey, buddy?"

He lifted a collar and leash off the hook beside the sliding door, the one he always kept on hand in case he wanted to take Tucker for a walk when Justin wasn't around.

Tucker barked, his tail wagging, then sat at Derek's feet panting.

"You like that idea?" He crouched down to Tucker's level, scratching his chin. "No running off, so you need to wear this." Derek held the collar out, and Tucker's tail stopped wagging, but he didn't put up a fuss when Derek fastened it around his neck.

Derek could have driven his truck over to Justin's, but the walk would give him a few minutes to work off some frustration. He'd spent almost six hours in the emergency room having his broken nose reset. He smirked, rubbing his head. Justin knew how to throw a hell of a punch. He'd been on the receiving end many, many times over the years.

He circled Justin's house, but there weren't any lights on, and Justin's car wasn't parked out front. He pulled the keys from his pocket and let himself in through the back door. Tucker headed straight for his food dish, then turned back and stared at Derek, eyes blinking.

It was empty.

"What?" Derek grabbed a bag of dog food from the larder and set it on the floor. "You think I'm going to feed you any of this?" He laughed. The look in Tucker's eyes, the most sorrowful dog of all time. "Okay, fine." He spilled a scoop of food into the dog dish, then stepped back, letting the suspense build as Tucker was made to wait, his teeth chattering.

"Okay, go!"

The food was gone within seconds.

"Did you taste any of that?" He ruffled the fur on Tucker's head. "I have to go. If your dad finds me in his kitchen, he is not going to be happy."

The last thing he needed was a black eye in addition to the broken nose. As it was, the swelling and bruising were radiating up to include both eyes.

He stepped out onto the front porch and zipped his jacket up under his chin to protect himself from the cold wind that swept through the forest at night.

As he stood there, something caught his eye. The snaps and

rushes of the wind had made a mess of Justin's stars-and-stripes flying from the porch's corner post.

He headed for the steps. It only took a second to release the flag. It immediately took to the wind, fluttering as free as the country it was meant to represent. Its presence on Justin's home was paramount to him. Justin had always been incredibly patriotic. The loss of his brother had hit him hard, but it hadn't deterred Justin's immense pride in their nation.

Derek brushed his fingers along the edge of the fabric and gripped the hewn-log banister beneath it. It had been a relief to hear that Breanne had followed through and moved back home.

He tapped on the wood of a nearby post. He needed to make a decision. Stay or go. Justin had made it quite clear he didn't want him around, but he needed to try one more time. He needed to talk to Justin, to see if they could repair their relationship.

He wandered to the far edge of the porch, making a deal with himself. If Justin were still out after a half-hour had passed, he'd go home.

He paced for a moment, and then took a seat, leaning back in a bench swing. He'd never noticed it hanging there before. He rubbed the armrest with his hand. It must've been. It was worn from age and use. Maybe Justin had found it at an estate sale, or it might have been his granny's.

The swing propelled forward as he leaned back. Bracing it with the heels of his boots, Derek looked out at the stars from beneath the overhang, wondering if Justin was somewhere he could see them as well. They'd spent many hours in their youth lying in the grass in silence, staring up at the constellations so close their hands often brushed against each other's.

He closed his eyes.

Lying there, he'd felt it—the heat. The charged connection between them, but he'd been oblivious to the fact Justin might have felt it too.

Derek stroked his nose and pulled the edges of the sticky

bandages away enough to loosen the splint. The throbbing and pinching subsided somewhat. Enough that he could close his eyes and not be disturbed by the sensation of an elephant standing on his face.

Damn impressive right hook.

Derek looked at his watch. He'd been waiting for Justin for over an hour, and there was still no sign of him. He'd stayed longer than he'd planned.

The sound of Justin's gravel driveway crunching under the pressure of tires alerted him to a change in that status. He stood and approached the top step as a taxi crept up the driveway.

Justin crawled out, nearly landing on all fours, dropping bits of change and balled up pieces of paper onto the driveway as he dug around in his pockets for the money to pay the cab driver.

"Justin," Derek said as he thundered down the steps and skirted around him. "I'll handle that. You go on into the house."

Justin slipped and fell to one knee, then righted himself. "You can't tell me what to do." He swerved and grabbed ahold of a post at the base of the steps. "I know what's best for me."

Derek thanked the driver and strode down the walkway to gather Justin up. He helped him navigate the steps and kicked the front door closed behind them with his foot.

"Did you have a good night?" Derek asked as he removed Justin's boots for him and directed him toward the stairs to the second floor.

"It was fucking awesome." Justin tripped on the first step but saved himself by grasping the handrail. "I met a guy."

Derek grunted. "Oh—"

"Not that kind of guy. A straight guy."

"Even better." Derek threw open Justin's bedroom door, helped him onto the bed, and removed his jeans. He pulled each sock off as well and threw the entire lot of clothes onto the top of Justin's dresser.

"Does *straight guy* have a name?" he asked.

Justin giggled and flopped over into the center of the bed, bringing the comforter with him. "Kadema. His wife says he talks too much."

Derek raised an eyebrow. "And does he?"

"Nah, he's great. We're going to be good friends." Justin tucked his face into a pillow. "He told me so."

Derek grinned. "Did he now?"

Justin rolled back, reached for Derek, and pulled at Derek's sleeve until he sat down on the bed beside him. "He says I shouldn't have hit you."

"I think I like your friend." Derek brushed a hand through Justin's hair. His heart felt as though it was melting when Justin nuzzled deeper into the caress. "Justin …"

"Shh…" Justin gripped onto Derek's arm. "I'm trying to hear what my brain is saying." He shifted closer to Derek. "I do ..."

Derek looked down at Justin. "You do what?"

Justin cleared his throat. "I should have said …but I didn't." He stared up at Derek and clutched the bedding, attempting to sit up. "Oh my god! Look at your face!"

"It's fine." Derek snorted, laughing. "Not like you've never broken my nose before."

"I did that to you?"

"No, I made the rounds today asking guys if they were in love with me." Derek shrugged. "This is what it got me."

Justin relaxed back into the bedding and shook his finger at Derek. "See, you're doing that thing again. You can be a complete asshole sometimes, but I'm in love with you anyway."

"Justin—"

"No," Justin said, then yawned and shoved at Derek to get him off the bed. "Go home before I do something stupid."

Derek stood at the edge of the bed as Justin drifted off. His heart was telling him to climb in behind Justin and hold him—to inhale the earthy scent of his hair. To feel the curve of Justin's back pressed against his chest. To kiss the soft hairs on the back of Justin's neck.

To fall asleep to the sound of his gentle breathing.

Justin stirred, mumbled something, and smacked his lips together.

Derek leaned in and ran his fingers along the hair behind Justin's ear. He was so peaceful looking as he slept, nothing at all like the terror he'd witnessed in Justin's voice the night he'd been assaulted.

He flinched as an image clawed into his mind. Justin naked and frantic, screaming and sobbing, trying to escape Nick's thrusting hips.

His ass taking the full length of another man's cock.

A shiver of revulsion ran up Derek's spine, and he backed away.

I'm sorry.

I can't do this with you.

I can't keep torturing myself like this.

Chapter Sixteen

The *cold kitchen* didn't look as interesting as the one he'd been working in for the past two months.

And to make matters worse, Kadema's rotation had landed him in the bakery for the next few weeks, so he was on his own.

Justin leaned up against the counter, perusing the different food items in front of him while he waited for the instructor to begin. It appeared they were going to be making a lot of sandwiches.

Probably for the cafeteria.

He appreciated the need for practical experience, but he was beginning to feel as though the culinary course was a ploy for free labor. He flipped open his textbook to a section on cheeses, becoming absorbed in the information. Despite the occasional doldrums, they *were* learning plenty of useful things, but he was feeling a little exposed being on his own.

It was making him antsy ...and a bit grumpy.

He looked across the counter at a guy he'd noticed during the culinary course's orientation. A guy who had been devouring him with his eyes since he'd walked into the room.

"Were you in the bakery last rotation?" Justin asked, deciding to take Kadema's approach and be the one to initiate conversations.

Especially if they're as hot as this guy.

"No, I've had the unique pleasure of spending much of my time learning how to cut up dead animals."

Justin grinned.

Damn.

The guy's eyes had taken on a mischievous sparkle.

"Lucky you," he said as he extended his hand. "I'm Justin."

"Kevin."

A tingle ran up Justin's spine when Kevin didn't release his hand right away, instead brushing his thumb back and forth across Justin's wrist while watching him intently.

Justin's tongue slipped out, and he licked his lips in response. A bad habit he'd picked up, but one that had served him well.

"Did you want to grab a coffee after class today?" Kevin asked as he relinquished his hold on Justin's hand. There was a hunger in Kevin's eyes that gave away his real intention. Justin knew coffee wasn't on the menu. He was.

And it was damn tempting.

"Can I get back to you after class?" Justin asked.

Kevin touched his hand again. "Sure thing, hon."

Justin picked up some worksheets to fan his face, there was so much sexual tension pulsing between them across the table, Justin was considering heading home with the guy.

He shivered.

Things were different now. He'd promised himself he wasn't going to hook up with random guys anymore. Consent, equality, respect, trust, and safety were going to govern his decisions about whom he slept with from now on. Plus, the thought of being intimate with anyone other than Derek felt like he'd be cheating on him.

It wasn't over between them. Not yet.

He tapped his pen on the table a few times. He hadn't seen Derek since the day he'd registered for the culinary course. The same day Derek had helped him to bed after a night of excessive alcohol consumption. The details were fuzzy, but he was certain he'd told Derek he was still in love with him. After that, Derek had been impossible to reach. He'd run away from him again, even though Derek had been at his house, waiting for him to come home that night.

Something was scaring Derek, holding him back, and

causing him to flip back and forth. It was likely the memory of the assault, but then why had Derek approached him in the parking lot that day after stalking him for weeks. Why had Derek asked him if he was still in love with him? Had he changed his mind? Had he decided he wanted to be with him after all?

Justin had decided he didn't want to know. He didn't want to hand Derek his heart again, only to have Derek stomp on it and run, so he'd told Derek he didn't even want to be friends with him anymore. He'd decided to be the one to run this time, to protect himself.

He'd wandered close to Derek's property a few times when he'd been heading for the hills for a walk. Sometimes he caught a glimpse of Derek, but most often not. Trekking through the woods on his own, without the sound of Derek's voice beside him, felt wrong. Even Tucker had hesitated a few times, looking toward Derek's house, expecting Derek to join them.

Justin glanced up at Kevin, and gripped the edge of the counter, sweating and shaking as an image invaded his mind. Kevin naked, sucking his cock ...begging him to fuck him.

Shut up, bitch.

Nick, pinning him down, grunting, and swearing in his ear.

He gasped for breath as the room spiraled and tilted.

That's it, bitch. Beg for it.

Justin's hands slipped from gripping the counter as everything went black. The *crack* as his head hit the floor startled him, but he kept his eyes shut for a moment.

He attempted to roll over, but there were hands on him, muffled voices telling him he was all right but not to get up quite yet.

He reached out with his hand, unsure if the voices were real.

Just stay down for a minute.

It'll pass.

After what seemed hours, he rolled onto his side but had no idea where he was. The white tile flooring stretched out before him, cold against his cheek, unfamiliar.

He scanned the room.

The school ...right.

A surge of lucidity had Justin scrambling to his feet. He clutched his head, using his fingers to feel for any blood or lumps. There were neither.

This wasn't the first time he'd passed out. Sometimes, Nick rampaging through his mind was too much. And his body would succumb.

The episodes were happening less and less often now, which gave him hope the invasions might stop one day.

"Are you going to be all right?" Kevin gripped Justin's shoulder. "I can take you to the hospital."

"No, that's all right," Justin said, shaking his head. "I've had plenty of knocks on the head. This is nothing. My ears aren't even ringing."

"Are you sure?"

"Yeah, I'm good." Justin gathered up his books, wishing he were away from the school and at home. Except, he didn't want to be at home either. He didn't want to be alone. There was only one place he wanted to be. And only one person he wanted to be with.

And that's where he was headed, whether Derek liked it or not. It was time for both of them to stop playing games. It was time for them to stop running from each other.

Derek cleared the last of the debris away from the backside of his house. He'd torn down the deck attached to the kitchen. It was circa nineteen seventy, and rotten right down to the cement pillars it was perched upon. He tossed the last piece of rotten wood into the dumpster he'd rented.

That's enough.

He wiped the back of a dirty glove across his brow. Despite the cold, he was happy to be outside being productive, but it was late. The light would be fading soon.

Derek turned when he heard a car door slam.

"Hey, Justin," he called out as he trudged up the short path to his driveway. They hadn't seen each other in months. Aside from his drunken confession, Justin had been quite clear about them ending their friendship. The next morning he'd received a text message from Justin with an explicit plea for space. And he'd promised himself he wouldn't go anywhere he might see Justin.

Not knowing why Justin had shown up at his house unexpectedly after that amount of time had him feeling uneasy.

"How are your classes going?" he asked.

"Fantastic." Justin leaned back against his car, his eyes sparkling in the fading light. His smile as always, contagious. "I love it. I do."

Derek tucked a grin behind a clenched fist.

"What's so funny?" Justin asked.

"Nothing." Derek bit at his bottom lip. "I've never seen you look so excited about something. It looks good on you."

"Thanks. It's been an amazing experience. I wake up every morning feeling optimistic." Justin drummed his fingers on the roof of his car. "I'm sorry for dropping in on you, but I didn't want to be alone. I had a bit of an incident—accident today."

"What happened?" Derek pulled his gloves off and stuffed them in his coat pocket.

"I passed out. Smacked my head pretty good."

"What?" Derek strode right up to Justin and ran his fingers through Justin's hair, looking for any sign of injury. It had been automatic. When he didn't feel anything, he stepped back and slipped his hands into his pockets. "You didn't go to see a doctor, did you?"

"Nah," Justin said. "I've had worse." He laughed. "Remember that damn beam. I thought for sure I was a goner. Knocked a couple of numbers off my IQ score for sure."

Why are you here?

Why are you really here?

Derek's heart thrummed faster as Justin's face lit up, his hands accentuating the bits of the story he felt needed emphasizing as he filled him in on the details of his culinary courses. His lips full and flushed. His eyes the lightest shade of blue imaginable, darkening to a seductive shade of navy in the fading light.

He clenched his hands closed, then opened them.

Closed. Open. Closed. Open.

He became fixated on what lay beneath Justin's clothing. His rugged, powerful shoulders driving the movement of his arms. His solid, muscular thighs. The flat of his stomach accentuating the protrusion of his hipbones, and the tempting trail of light hair descending. A path he'd dreamed of tracing downward with his tongue. And Justin's ass. He needed to clutch it within his hands.

His willpower was taking a beating.

Derek almost groaned aloud as his cock hardened. He'd seen much of Justin's upper torso and thighs over the years when the heat became too much to bear. Even his ass, and sometimes his cock, when they'd taken off into the forest to go skinny-dipping in the nearby swimming hole.

This was different.

Since then, they'd both expressed their desire for one another, acknowledging their regret for not speaking up. For not sharing a sleeping bag. For not making love to each other.

"Derek?"

"Sorry, what?" Derek blinked his eyes, refocusing on Justin's face.

"I said I have something I want to talk to you about."

"And what would that be?" Derek kicked at the stones near his feet, directing his gaze away from Justin. He was agonizingly certain he knew where this conversation was headed.

Please don't.

Derek's pulse thundered in his ears as panic coursed through his body. He fixed his attention on the ground and swore under his breath as he fought to contain an army of tears that threatened to spill. The last thing he wanted to do was cause Justin any more pain.

Justin, please don't—

"I'm in love with you, Derek," Justin said as he stepped in close enough to Derek for the toes of his paint-spattered work boots to scuff up against Derek's. "I've tried to move on without you. I have, but it's not possible. You're a part of me, and you'll always be."

The tears Derek had been holding back, escaped down his cheeks. Justin would always be a part of him as well. The only part that had ever mattered to him.

Justin cupped Derek's face with both hands and raised it until their eyes met. He brushed away the tears decorating Derek's skin. "I love you, and I want us to be together."

Derek's lips parted as though to speak, but he remained silent. There was so much love in Justin's eyes, searching his for the love he would surely find there. His resolve wavered.

He released a pathetic sigh. "Justin, I can't."

"What do you mean, *can't*?"

"I just can't." Derek turned from Justin and took off down the nearest path headed away from his house. Justin hurried to catch up with him.

"Where are we going?" Justin shouted.

Derek stopped abruptly and pivoted. "*We* are not going anywhere. *I* am going into the bush to collect some firewood." He started toward the treed area at the end of his property. He needed to create as much distance as possible between them.

"Oh no, you don't." Justin jogged down the path, grabbed ahold of Derek's shoulder, and clutched tight to his thick work jacket, stopping Derek's retreat. "You are not running away from me this time." He wrenched Derek around to face him.

"Don't." Derek yanked his arm from Justin's grasp and started down the path again. He turned his collar up against the cold and picked up speed, jogging down a steep incline until he reached an area with less of a slope. He turned back to see if Justin was still following.

The full weight of Justin's body slammed against his chest, and he lost his footing. He felt himself become airborne for a second before his back slammed against the ground.

Derek scrambled to get away, but Justin tackled him and knocked him to the ground a second time. This time Justin pinned Derek down with the weight of his body.

"Don't you dare fucking run," Justin reiterated, and then descended upon Derek's mouth.

Derek hesitated, then relaxed into the tender warmth of Justin's lips, his heart hammering in his chest. He'd spent most of their time together tempted to kiss them, to feel the quickening of Justin's breath mixed with his own. The kiss was unexpectedly soft, tentative, and unsure.

Justin broke away from Derek's mouth for a moment and stared down at him, his chest heaving against Derek's in a shallow but rapid rise and fall.

He changed his hold on Derek. Slowly at first, then shifted the position of his legs.

A simmering heat erupted between them.

Derek wrapped his hands around the back of Justin's head and pulled him closer, refusing to release his lips—his mouth …his tongue. He wanted all of it. Giving and taking as they immersed themselves in a depth of passion neither one of them had anticipated.

Justin pulled at Derek's jacket, seeking a way in.

Wait, no.

He couldn't allow this to go any further. Derek grabbed Justin's shoulders, stopping him, then rolled, taking Justin with him until Justin was beneath him.

"Justin, I'm sorry, but I can't do this with you."

Justin grabbed ahold of Derek's coat when Derek tried to

pull away. He kept Derek's lips hovering above his own by holding tight to Derek's collar. "I'm not letting you run."

"Please." Derek broke Justin's grip on his coat and attempted to stand, but Justin wrapped his legs around him, holding him in place.

"Cut it out," Derek said. "Let me up."

"No." Justin squeezed his legs tight around Derek's thighs. "Not until you tell me what's going through your mind." He angled his hips up, thrusting them against Derek's waning erection as he ran his hands onto Derek's ass. "What are you so damned afraid of?"

Derek gazed off into the darkening forest.

"I don't want to talk about it," he said. "I don't want to hurt you."

"You're hurting me now by not telling me." Justin stroked his hand up Derek's back and squeezed his shoulder. "I need to know what's making you run."

Derek pulled his upper body away from Justin's embrace, breathing easier as Justin released him. He lay down beside him and stared up into the barren trees above. "I can't get the sound of you screaming and sobbing out of my head." He covered his eyes with his hand. "And the sight of you lying there in the tent. Knowing you'd had another man inside you …"

Justin peeled himself off the ground and headed toward the driveway.

"Justin, wait." Derek leaped up. That had come out all wrong. Or maybe it hadn't. Justin had asked him what was going through his mind, and he'd told him the truth.

He caught up with Justin and stopped him from getting into his car.

"I didn't mean to—"

"Save it," Justin interrupted. "I knew you wouldn't want me. I just hadn't realized the extent of your disgust in me."

"No—wait." Derek reached for Justin's face, but Justin

knocked his hand away and tried to climb into his car. Derek held the door shut. "It's not that I don't want you."

"Then what is it?" Justin pressed the heel of his hand to his temple. "Because it sounds to me like that's exactly what it is. When you look at me, all you see is what happened that night."

"That's not true. I see so much more than that."

"Bullshit. If you saw more than that in me, you wouldn't be acting this way. You wouldn't be chasing me off right now. You'd be willing to work through the challenges we'd be facing together." He wiped a stream of tears from his cheek.

"All the years we've spent together, gone," Justin added. "Like they never mattered."

"Please don't say that."

"It's true. Even though we've always been closer than any other couple we've ever known."

"We were never a couple, Justin."

"Weren't we?" Justin played with a few of the dark curls framing Derek's face. "We may as well have been. We've rarely left each other's side for the past sixteen years." He brushed the back of his hand along the scruff at Derek's jaw. "Sixteen years, Derek. That's a long time for two people to remain together."

Derek sighed and looked skyward. "I don't see how I'll ever be able to move past what happened to you. I'm sorry."

Justin's brow creased. "So, you're going to let him continue—raping me, is that it?"

"What? No."

"You are. Except now, this ongoing assault, it's so much worse because I know you've had feelings for me all along. And yet, you keep throwing me back into that tent with him anyway."

"That's not fair." Derek stepped away from Justin but found himself wanting to reach out. "I would never let him hurt you again."

"Then don't. Don't let him keep hurting me."

Derek's pulse quickened. He wanted to wrap his hand around

the back of Justin's neck, haul him in, and attack his mouth.

Savage …and so damn heated.

He stopped his retreat.

The thought of keeping his distance from Justin a single second more, despite everything that had happened, was no longer an option. He never wanted Justin to find himself in that tent again.

Derek closed the gap between them.

Chapter Seventeen

Justin took a trembling breath, his fingers embedded deep in the mess of curls at the nape of Derek's neck. He drew Derek closer as they both struggled to kick their boots off without letting go of one another. Their coats discarded before they'd even reached the garage.

Derek's mouth had sought to devour him, biting, and tasting—heating his flesh. It was a side of Derek he'd never witnessed before. Being Derek's best friend for the past sixteen years never could have prepared him for the level of sexual aggression Derek could unleash.

It had shocked him at first, the way Derek had overpowered him, his raw sexual desire bearing down on him, possessing him, pinning him to his car—compelling him to surrender.

And he had.

He'd turned himself over to Derek without reservation. He'd come to trust this man with his life over the years. There was no reason not to trust him now.

Justin tipped his head to one side, giving Derek unrestricted access to the thrumming pulse at his throat, but it wasn't enough. Justin stripped his shirt off over his head and guided Derek down to tease the hard nubs his nipples had become due to the freezing temperature inside the garage.

He backed up against a workbench, unable to maintain his balance as Derek flicked and sucked at them, then kissed his way down the center of his body.

"Fuck." Justin arched his back and groaned as Derek shimmied his jeans down far enough to bite and suck at the protruding bones of his hips.

Derek undid the button of his jeans.

No—wait.

Stop.

Justin steadied his breathing, placed his hands along Derek's jawline, and tipped Derek's face to look up at him. There was no explanation needed.

Derek rose to his feet, cupped Justin's face, and immersed himself in the depths once more, the meeting of their lips coming in heated waves. Derek backed away, breathless, then tugged on the waistband of Justin's jeans, pulling him through the door into the house.

"Can't have you freezing to death," he said.

"Hold on." Justin hopped along, gripping tight to Derek's shoulder as he fought to remove his remaining boot. "I thought you were going to hit me when you came charging at me out there."

Derek's warm rumbling laugh filled the space between them.

"It crossed my mind."

Justin kicked his boot free. "What changed it?"

Derek grabbed Justin, spun him around, and growled against Justin's neck as he backed his ass up against the nearest wall in the back hallway.

The heat of his breath enveloped Justin's throat, restraining him there.

"I decided," he said, "I'd rather see you naked than laid out flat on my driveway."

Justin smirked. "Naked on your driveway never occurred to you?"

"Maybe next time."

"I might hold you to that." Justin peeled Derek's shirt off over his head and ran his hands down Derek's muscular chest.

Derek raked his hands up Justin's back and into his hair, then gripped tight. The sting of the aggressive hold amplified the ache building within Justin's body.

An ache to have Derek writhing and shuddering beneath him.

Justin propelled Derek across the hallway, forced him against the opposite wall, and pinned him there. He brushed Derek's hair aside and took a moment to inhale the scent of Derek's skin.

It was intoxicating, fresh winter air, cedar, and the salty essence of strenuous labor.

He moved his hands around to Derek's ass and hauled him closer. The extent of Derek's arousal pressing against his own had Justin recapturing Derek's mouth.

He unlatched Derek's buckle and undid the button of his jeans.

"Whoa," Derek said, stopping Justin with a gentle hand. "Slow down a second."

"I don't want to." Justin brushed Derek's hand away and took ahold of Derek's zipper.

"I'm serious." Derek grabbed Justin's hand, squeezing it so Justin couldn't break free. "We need to have a conversation, okay?"

Justin nodded. "Yeah, I know." He placed both hands on his hips. A look of deep concern had descended upon Derek's expression. The last time he'd seen it, in the hospital when he'd awoken from his coma. He leaned against the wall behind him.

"There is nothing I want more right now," Derek said, "than to strip you bare, and make love to you." He placed a tentative kiss on Justin's lips and lingered for a moment, then pressed his forehead to Justin's. "I need to know if you're going to be all right."

"I don't know." Justin looked away toward the end of the hallway. "I honestly don't." The only person who'd touched his body since the assault had been his massage therapist. It had taken months to progress from the therapist placing her unmoving hands on his back while he cried for the entire hour, to the point where he was able to tolerate a somewhat relaxing session.

This was different. This was Derek.

"Justin." Derek touched Justin's face and stroked his cheek until Justin faced him again. "You need to know, even if we *never* go any further than this, I'm not going to love you any less."

Justin's face flushed, and he smiled.

Derek had finally—at long fucking last—told him he loved him. It had been phrased differently than a proclamation of love, but he wasn't giving the distinction any weight. The look in Derek's eyes as he'd spoken those words was all he needed to clarify the message.

He hooked his fingers in the loops of Derek's jeans, drawing him near and devoured Derek's mouth once more, before leading him down the hallway toward the bedroom.

He backed up until he was at the edge of the mattress, and lay back, his hands entwined behind his head, and his feet still maintaining contact with the floor.

"Are you sure," Derek asked as he stood between Justin's legs, his own legs pressed against the mattress. He ran his hands up and down Justin's thighs.

Justin undid the button of his jeans and unzipped them.

"Does that answer your question?"

Derek growled, maintaining eye contact with Justin as he pulled on the pant legs of Justin's jeans and removed them. Justin's socks were the next things to hit the floor.

He lifted one of Justin's feet and held it in his hands. "Say stop if you want me to. No questions asked."

Justin nodded and then erupted into a shocked stream of gasping breaths. He stared at the ceiling, his balls escalating from tingling to aching within seconds. He coughed as he grasped the bedding on either side of him, twisting it within his hands.

He was sure his eyes were rolling back in his head as Derek bit and sucked at his ankle, the top of his foot, his heel …his toes.

No one had ever.

Derek licked a winding path up to the sensitive skin behind his knee.

"Oh—god." Justin reached for Derek's hair; the added sensation of Derek's thick scruff upon his skin had created an entirely new level of ecstasy.

The primal part of him wanted Derek to continue, but another part of him was legitimately concerned he might pass out from overstimulation.

A giggle escaped his lips before he could subdue it. Derek had taken to teasing the bottom of his foot with his tongue.

"Enough, enough," Justin said, gasping and laughing. "Oh my god, why didn't we do this sooner."

He slapped his palm to his forehead. Derek had released the hold on his foot and risen to his feet. Silent. Derek pinched the ridge of his nose and looked away

You are such a dumbass, Leary.

"That came out all wrong," Justin said. "Yes, maybe if we'd hooked up in the tent that night, everything might have turned out different, but we didn't."

He reached for the nearest pocket on Derek's jeans and pulled him closer. "I only meant we should have started playing around from—I don't know ...the first day we met or something."

Derek appeared to relax, then shot Justin a sly look.

"Then I would've missed out on all those years of practice."

Justin fell back, snorting, his arms flung out to his sides. "Don't remind me." He lifted his head from the bed. "What else have you been *practicing*?"

"Well ..." Derek rushed at Justin, leaped onto the bed, and straddled him, his hands prepared to support himself on either side of Justin's head.

Justin thrust his hand up and slammed it against Derek's chest, stopping him.

Derek rushing at him while they'd been outside had been different. He'd been standing. Able to get away if he needed to.

Here, lying flat out, vulnerable …the memory of Nick overpowering him had come on fast. The panic had flooded his body as soon as Derek appeared above him, the scent of damp tent fabric, seeping into his mind.

Derek was quick to climb off, allowing Justin to sit up.

"Fuck, I'm sorry," Derek said as he paced to the far side of the room, then back again. "I wasn't thinking."

"No, you couldn't have known." Justin leaned forward, placed his head in his hands, and stared down at the floor. "I didn't even know."

He straightened up and brushed his hand back and forth across the bedding beside him.

This was the opening he was supposed to be watching for, an opportunity to explain what his reactions might be—a step that required a level of trust in his partner. Of which he had plenty where Derek was concerned. Plus, he knew Derek would be receptive. The loving concern in Derek's eyes as he'd leaped off the bed had confirmed that.

"There are some things you need to know," Justin said. "Reactions I might have. Reactions you might spot the warning signs for, even before I know I'm heading toward them."

"When you flinched in the garage. Was that …"

"Yeah, you …your mouth …a bit too close," Justin responded. "In the tent, I …Nick."

"Don't. You don't need to explain."

"I know, but …"

Justin paused to rework what he was going to say. Practicing in the support group was one thing. Speaking to the man you loved, disclosing adverse reactions to something as intimate as making love to each other, was embarrassing.

"Justin?" Derek's hand came to rest on Justin's shoulder.

"I'm finding this a little difficult." Justin chewed at his bottom lip, and then released it. "My triggers, they could be anything. Something I see, smell, feel …even taste. I just need to breathe through them. And know I'll have your understanding if I hesitate."

He contemplated telling Derek why he'd passed out at the school today. Why imagining a guy in his class naked had caused him to faint ...why he'd been imagining a random guy naked in the first place. He decided against it.

"What else?" Derek asked.

"Disassociation. If you see me drifting off somewhere, stop whatever you're doing."

"Stop ...that's it?" Derek scrubbed at the scruff along his jawline. "Is it all right if I hold you?"

Justin sucked a cleansing breath in through his nose and pressed the tip of his tongue against his teeth as he exhaled in an effort to control his emotions. There were few ways to describe what he was experiencing. During his group therapy sessions, he'd depicted Derek as an egotistical, manipulative prick who didn't care about him or his feelings. He couldn't have been more wrong.

"Justin, if that's not a good idea, you can tell me."

"No, it is a good idea. I'd love for you to hold me."

"All right." Derek stood, then undid his jeans and dropped them to the floor along with his socks. He tapped Justin's knee to get him to move over and lie down, then stretched out beside him. "How's your head? How hard did you hit that floor at school?"

Justin ran his fingers through his hair, searching for any swelling. He didn't even have a headache. Not yet anyway. It would probably sneak up on him in a few hours.

He placed his hands on his stomach.

"It seems fine."

"Good."

The silence that followed almost sent Justin into a fit of giggles. They'd never once run out of things to say to each other before.

"Did you catch the Fury game last week?" Derek said.

Justin laughed as he shifted closer to Derek. "You hate

baseball."

"True. We could talk about renovation work if you want, but I'd rather not."

Justin ran his fingers through the dark hair of Derek's chest and twirled a few strands within them. He swept his hand across Derek's stomach, then down.

"Maybe we don't have to talk about anything."

A faint groan from Derek was all the answer he needed. Justin pushed himself up on one elbow and brushed the flat of his hand along the outline of Derek's cock beneath his briefs.

It responded to his touch immediately.

"Fuck," Justin whispered. Waking up this morning, he never would have imagined he'd be in Derek's bed by nightfall, with no intention of sleeping, stroking Derek's cock with his hand until the full length of Derek's thick shaft was visible as it pressed against the tight fabric.

Justin slipped his hand beneath the band of Derek's briefs and dragged them off Derek's hips, then rose up onto his knees, and hauled them down past Derek's thighs.

"Kick them off," he directed Derek.

Derek took ahold of Justin's arm and used his feet to remove his briefs. He ran his hand up to Justin's shoulder, around to the back of his neck, and pulled Justin down to his mouth, his grip intensifying as their tongues engaged in a struggle for dominance.

Justin hummed against Derek's mouth as he descended along the center of Derek's body with his hand. Derek's muscles jumped and twitched beneath his touch, his hips undulating.

Begging.

He took Derek's cock in his hand and stroked it, firm and slow.

Derek arched his back, groaning. Sighing. He grabbed ahold of Justin's arm and clung to it, his fingers making deep imprints in the flesh of Justin's biceps. Justin sucked in a breath. The strength of Derek's hand bit into him, but the pain was not unwelcome.

He glanced up toward Derek's face, the familiar features he'd studied more than a thousand times, transformed by lust and need.

Derek's eyes were closed, his thick dark lashes fluttering. His mouth open. The tip of his tongue slipping in and out to lick his flushed lips. It was a sight he'd never thought he'd be the one eliciting from Derek. Somewhere in the back of his mind over the years, he'd thought it would be awkward between them if they ever hooked up.

It wasn't.

Derek's growing arousal, guided by his touch, felt instinctive and natural. As if they'd been lovers their entire lives.

Justin drew Derek's foreskin tight to his body, fully exposing the glistening, crimson head.

Fucking beautiful.

He licked his lips, wishing he knew whether the sensation of Derek's cock filling his mouth would set off a bout of panic. He decided against finding out, but the shimmer of precum was too much to resist.

He caressed the thick ridge of Derek's cock-head with his thumb and dipped it into the drooling slit. Collecting a taste, he slipped his thumb into his mouth, savoring the essence of the clear, slick liquid as he stared intently into Derek's eyes.

He licked his lips.

"Damn, Justin," Derek whispered, then shifted his grip on Justin's arm, clenching and releasing, digging his nails in, and pulling at Justin to return to him.

Justin left his position at Derek's side and climbed atop him. He placed one of his legs between Derek's, took hold of Derek's mouth, and dove into it.

The shimmer of quivering heat filled Justin's body. He clenched the pillow behind Derek's head, his arousal surging as Derek's tongue began a thorough search of his mouth, seeking out any remnants of the precum he'd stolen from him.

He rocketed up, giving Derek as much access as he needed. *Oh god yes.*

The intensity increased, leaving them both breathless.

It seemed inhibitions were not going to be an issue between them. Justin's mind paged through future scenarios as Derek's tongue ran along the surface of his teeth.

Derek sucked on Justin's bottom lip as he released it. "You are one tasty guy, Leary."

Justin smirked. "Are you sure that's not you?"

"Possibly." Derek waggled his eyebrows at Justin. "We'll have to revisit that theory some other time." He stroked the hair above Justin's ear. "Are you planning on sampling anything else?"

Justin snorted. "If you're good."

Derek smirked out a cocky half-smile. "I haven't had any complaints."

"You seriously are an asshole sometimes." Justin ran his fingers up into the thick dark curls of Derek's hair. He'd lain awake many nights staring at those curls, fantasizing about touching them without waking Derek, but he'd never been brave enough to try.

"Damn, you're hot," Justin whispered as he stared down into Derek's eyes. They looked different. Electrified. Afire somehow. Derek smirking up at him made him smile.

"I'm sorry, what?" Derek said.

"Don't even start. I'm not taking it back. I think you're hot. Deal with it."

"Done." Derek wrapped his hand around the back of Justin's head, his rough, powerful grip positioned to keep Justin from retreating. "So, what are you going to do about it?"

Justin laced his fingers with Derek's and placed their linked hands above Derek's head. He ran his tongue along Derek's top lip, then immersed himself in the warmth, the taste, and the passion of Derek's lips, his cock grinding against Derek's thigh, undulating. Thrusting.

Derek's breath became labored and heated, further dampening the curls of his hair. Justin latched onto Derek's ear with his teeth and whispered his name.

And how much he wanted to fuck him some day.

Derek swore beneath his breath and freed his hands. He slipped them beneath the band of Justin's underwear and grasped at Justin's ass, his hands rough and brusque against Justin's skin.

He set the pace, forcing Justin to rock against him, harder and faster.

As Derek undulated his hips with increasing urgency, his breath quickening, Justin became frantic to remove the remaining layer of material between them. Derek's cock had been riding his thigh, skin to skin since he'd climbed on top of him.

He hauled at the band of his underwear and eventually managed to slip them off.

"You all good?" Derek whispered.

Justin smirked against Derek's throat. "I am now."

He shifted atop Derek, biting his shoulders, his neck, anything that would cause Derek to continue making the most incredible sounds.

Lust driven, throaty, and low like rolling thunder.

Derek wrapped his arms around Justin. He grasped at his shoulders, then moved down to his ass, and back up again as their cocks seeped, slicking up the skin between them.

Justin picked up his pace, grinding against Derek, panting, his face reddening.

The only thought in his mind—completion.

More.

Justin closed over Derek's mouth, wanting to capture the vibrations being exchanged between them as the shimmer of climax gathered in his balls.

He was about to cum.

That's the way you like it, isn't it, you fucking faggot.

Hard and fast up the ass.

"Shut up!" Justin spilled off Derek and scrambled away, almost falling off the far side of the bed. The smell of damp sleeping bag filled his nostrils.

Shut up, you little bitch.

Derek might hear you.

Justin punched the headboard, and leaped off the bed onto the floor, rage coloring and twisting his face. "Fuck! Fuck! Fuck!" His anger continued rising.

Derek crept to the edge of the bed.

"Justin, talk to me."

"Fuck!" Justin's fist struck a wall, breaking through the drywall, which pissed him off. He'd been hoping to hit a stud. White dust and pink insulation followed his hand's retreat.

"Please, tell me what happened." Derek attempted to grab Justin's arm, but Justin jerked away from Derek's touch, rampaged across the room, and swiped the pile of jeans off the floor.

He chucked them at the door, and then stopped to catch his breath.

"Are you done?" Derek asked.

Justin spun to face him. "Done? Yeah, pretty much." He collected his jeans off the floor. "I'm going home. Let's write this off as a mistake."

"What the hell are you talking about? A mistake. What we were doing back there ..." Derek pointed toward the bed. "Did not feel like a mistake."

Justin backed away, not wanting to engage in a shoving match with Derek. In a situation like this, when his temper was out of control, shoving could easily escalate to hitting.

"No, the whole thing is a mistake," he said. "I'm never going to be free of him."

"So, that's it between us?" Derek asked. "I thought we were going to work through this together?"

"There is no together. He didn't do this to *you*."

Justin approached the door but hesitated. It made absolutely no sense, considering, but if Derek blocked his way, held him, and told him he loved him, there was every possibility he would cave, and crawl back into bed with him.

Except, Derek, likely out of respect for his decision, remained where he was.

Chapter Eighteen

A construction job was a lame excuse to see Justin, but it had been over a week since Justin had taken off, and left him standing in his bedroom wondering what the hell had happened. He'd decided to give Justin some space, but he couldn't stand to be without him any longer.

He stopped at the edge of Justin's driveway and looked beyond the back corner of Justin's house. The light in Justin's workshop was on.

As he wandered closer, he saw Justin through the open double-doorway, sanding the headboard of a small bed. Justin's clothes were covered in fine dust, and he was humming to himself. The sound of Justin's voice carried straight through to his heart.

Derek stood there for a moment, watching Justin's expert hand turn raw, rough wood into something beautiful. When Justin brushed the sanding dust off the piece he'd been working on, Tucker awoke from his place on the floor and ran over to where Derek was standing.

"Hey, buddy," Derek said as he reached down to scratch Tucker's head. He squatted to give his ears a good rub. "What's your dad making? A bed for Brittany?"

Justin tossed the worn piece of sandpaper onto his workbench. "Karen was hoping I'd have it done for Brittany's birthday next month."

"It's beautiful."

"Thanks." Justin reached for a new piece of sandpaper, but Derek stepped in his way.

"We need to talk," Derek said.

Justin pushed Derek out of the way and snatched what he

needed off the workbench. "About what? I broke things off. There's nothing to talk about." He began sanding a side rail leaning against the wall. "He won't ever stop haunting me."

Derek advanced toward Justin, leaving him no way to escape. "In time, he will."

"Derek, I can't—"

"Can't what?" Derek trapped Justin against the wall. "Can't abandon me? Good because this time, I'm not letting *you* run."

He stroked his knuckles along Justin's jawline, the rough stubble setting off a chain reaction. "Every time we went camping, I wanted to tell you how I felt about you. And what I wanted to do with you to show you how much you meant to me, but I was scared. I was scared you'd reject me. I was scared you *wouldn't* reject me. I had no idea what I wanted." Derek traced Justin's lips with his fingers. "Except for one thing. I knew I wanted you. And I still do."

Justin sniffed and wiped a layer of sawdust from his cheek with his sleeve.

"I remember lying in bed the night you snuck out," he said. "Praying you'd take me up on my offer, and climb into bed with me. I would've let you do anything to me as long as you kissed me first. For some reason that was important to me. That somehow you kissing me would mean we weren't just hooking up. That we'd be boyfriends. That we'd be *making love*. Not just having sex."

Justin released a short exhalation of air and smiled.

"I was just a kid. We both were," he said. "It didn't seem so at the time, but we were. I don't think either one of us had any clue what we were feeling."

Derek sucked in a breath, then looked away as he mopped at a collection of tears with the heel of his hand. He'd known. He'd known exactly what he was feeling.

He took a deep breath. "I came over here to ask for your help."

"With what?"

"My deck."

"Your deck?"

"Yeah, those support posts are a pain to install by myself."

"Um ...okay. I suppose I could help you with that. I've finished this bed for today." Justin brushed his hands off on his pants. "I'll be over after I tidy up."

Derek tapped his hand on his pant leg. "Also, I have a flooring job at the Miller House sometime next month. I'd appreciate some help with that as well."

Justin smirked. "Okay—fine. I'll be there."

Derek tipped his head to one side, staring at the ground.

"What?" Justin asked.

"I don't know." Derek shrugged. "Are we back ..." He scuffed the toe of his boot through a pile of wood chips at his feet, dispersing them. He didn't want to assume.

"Are we back together?" Justin stared at Derek, then pulled off his gloves and threw them onto the workbench. His brow dipped. "Yeah, we could take another go at this."

Derek released the accumulation of breath that had become trapped in his chest. "Okay—good." Relief coursed through his body. He cleared his throat. "I'll see you over there."

"Wait." Justin rubbed the back of his neck. "I need to clear something off my mind. Something I should have told you."

He set his hand on the workbench. "My mom ...she has Alzheimer's."

Derek looked away toward his own house. "I know. Bree told me."

Justin picked at the edge of the compressed wood of the workbench and peeled off the loose pieces. "I wish she hadn't done that."

"She means well."

"I know." Justin brushed his hands together. "I should have been the one to tell you though."

Derek placed his hand on Justin's shoulder.

"You weren't ready. I get that."

I really get that.

Justin shot him a shy glance. "Thanks. I'll join you over there in a bit."

Justin took the plans Derek handed to him and rolled them out on the patio table. He placed a rock on each of the four corners to keep them from lifting in the wind and smoothed the paper out with his hands. The scope and originality of the deck Derek had designed was impressive.

"This is quite the project to take on all by yourself."

Derek stepped up beside Justin and nudged him. "I hadn't planned on doing it myself."

Oh really.

Derek was adorable when he was joking around, his warm brown eyes sparkling, mischievous, his lips turned up in a cheeky smile that made you want to lick them. "Are you keeping some construction workers in the basement I don't know about?"

Derek shrugged. "Maybe."

"Well, they can stay there for now," Justin said. "Where do you want to start?"

The rest of the afternoon went by faster than he would've preferred. Working with Derek felt like coming home. They moved together in unison with few words spoken between them, each knowing what the other was thinking.

The last post base was secured in place as the light disappeared from the sky. The yard only illuminated by the dim light spilling into the backyard from Derek's kitchen.

"I guess we should wrap it up," Derek said. "I can't see a damn thing."

"We can tackle the joists tomorrow after I get home from school." Justin wiped the back of his hand across his forehead. Working with Derek had brought back many memories. Good memories. Memories of a life he'd left behind. "I should head home."

"Oh ..." Derek removed his gloves, held them in one hand, and squeezed them within his fist. "I was hoping you'd stick around for a bit."

"I don't know." Justin kicked the toe of his boot against a pile of wood stacked near the house. "I need a shower ...and something to eat."

Dammit, Derek.

Stop looking at me like that.

Seeing the disappointed look on Derek's face had him reconsidering. He had told Derek he was willing to have another go at their relationship, and Derek would never press him to be intimate again until he was ready. Even if he never was. Derek had told him so.

Removing that aspect of their relationship made no sense though, considering how he felt about him. He wanted to feel that fire between them again.

"I suppose I could stick around for a while."

"Good—great." Derek studied the ground where he was standing, then glanced at his hand, where his gloves were still strangled tight in his fist. "We'll have to go in through the garage."

"I figured." Justin trekked after Derek up the steep incline to the garage. "Hey, maybe we could order pizza *later.*"

"Sure, I can do that right now, place an order," Derek said. "You can go ahead and jump in the shower."

Justin started down the hallway to the bathroom. "I said order the pizza *later*, dumbass," he whispered to himself.

"I heard that."

"Did you?" Justin bit his lip as a shiver ran up his spine. "And what are you going to do about it?" Derek's rumbling laugh coming up behind him started a heated tingle in his balls.

"Are you sure?" Derek asked as he followed Justin into the bathroom.

"I am if you are," Justin said. As he started up the shower, he took a moment to admire Derek's renovation work, transforming one of the ugliest bathrooms he'd ever set foot in.

Impressive.

"What do you think?" Derek asked as he stepped up behind Justin, wrapped his arms around Justin's body, and rested his chin on his shoulder.

"Pretty sweet. When did you do it?"

"Over the past few months ...while you were at school."

"I'm sorry."

"Why?" Derek kissed the back of Justin's neck as he massaged his shoulders. "Work is slow. It kept me busy."

"How slow?"

Derek smirked. "As slow as you want me to be."

"Slow." Justin turned and placed his hands on Derek's chest. "Really fucking slow."

Derek growled from deep within his chest, then stripped Justin's shirt off over his head. "I'll try my best." He pressed Justin up against the nearest wall and descended upon his throat.

Finally.

Justin hadn't been able to suppress memories of Derek's hunger for him. Day and night, reliving every kiss, every touch. Every response of Derek's body.

Justin ran his hands up into Derek's hair, reveling in the return of last week's passion. It was back. The heat, the desire. The need to possess him. He discarded the rest of his clothing and wrenched on the buckle of Derek's jeans.

"So much for slow," Derek said as he scrambled out of the jeans and shirt Justin was attempting to strip from his body.

"Shut up and get in here."

Justin pulled Derek into the shower, pressed him into the corner, and demanded Derek's mouth be returned to his. He slipped his hands onto Derek's ass as he stepped in closer to him. The water showering down on them ran in rivulets between their lips, slicking them up. Derek's dark wet curls clung to his skin. His cheeks, his neck, adorned.

Justin smoothed Derek's hair away from his eyes. His eyelashes were dewy and separated into distinct peaks. His deep brown eyes ignited with overtones of need.

Derek picked up a bar of soap and worked up a lather in his hands. He massaged Justin's shoulders, then leaned in and kissed him.

"You have all the control, okay?"

"Okay," Justin whispered, and then Derek turned him to face the corner of the shower stall and soaped up his back. He flinched when Derek's hands reached the base of his spine.

"You're all right. I've got you." Derek's chest pressed against his back as he kissed the sensitive skin at the base of Justin's neck. Justin steadied himself.

Breathe.

"Talk to me if you need to." Derek wrapped his arms around Justin and brought him closer, his hard cock making contact with Justin's body.

Justin reached back and latched on to Derek's thigh, his instinct telling him to flee.

"Do you want me to stop?" Derek whispered against his cheek.

Justin released Derek's thigh and shook his head no. The panic he was feeling had limited his ability to speak. He licked his lips, and exhaled, steady—slow. His best friend, the man he loved, was taking him places he never knew existed—places where love was so much more than just love.

There was a spiritual connection between them.

He reached back and ran his fingers through Derek's hair, relaxing as Derek's hands stroked and massaged his chest.

His breath caught as Derek withdrew from caressing his chest and torso, and headed for his thighs. He bit his lip to fight back the tears while reaching behind him to draw Derek's lips onto the back of his neck. There would never be anyone who knew him as intimately as Derek.

He closed his eyes, the continuous motion of not just anyone's hands, but Derek's, began a relaxation in him unprecedented since his assault.

Even as Derek's thick, hard cock pressed against him—sometimes moving smoothly along his spine, occasionally slipping between his thighs and nudging his balls ...he felt safe.

He turned and touched his forehead to Derek's, keeping eye contact with him as his fingers lingered in the coarse, wet hair of Derek's jawline and sideburns.

"There is so much I want to say to you," Justin said. "So much more than I love you." He cast his eyes downward. "I can't even ..."

"You don't need to." Derek rubbed his thumb across Justin's bottom lip, and kissed him. "I can feel it." He kissed Justin again. "I can't imagine life without you. I love you so much."

Justin met Derek's eyes, blinking, and then licked his lips, at peace.

That's all he needed to know.

Derek hauled Justin close to his body, and propelled him into the corner, Justin's back making contact with the cool tiles. "Remember, you're the one with all the control. You say stop, I stop."

Justin tried to speak but was unable. The aggression and fervor were back.

Derek was at his shoulders, his throat, his mouth. Every piece of flesh Derek touched set his body afire until he was panting for breath.

"More," Justin whispered and dug his hands into the flesh of Derek's ass. Derek responded, his hips undulating and grinding, almost lifting Justin off his feet.

Justin shared a trembling exchange of breath as Derek slipped his hand between them, and encased both their cocks.

Caressing his way up to Derek's shoulders with his hands, Justin grasped tight to him. The sensation of Derek's cock against his, slipping up …then back, exposing, then sheathing, left him feeling weak.

He placed his hand on the wall to balance them both.

"Derek," Justin whispered, his voice trembling, the word *bitch* rumbling to be released from the back of his mind.

"Don't panic. I have you." Derek angled his hips away and released his cock, leaving only Justin's within his grasp.

At first, Justin jumped, his breath convulsing from his chest, then a rush of passion overtook him, and he began fucking Derek's clenched hand.

He tipped his head back into the corner while staring up at the ceiling of the shower, his fingers clawing Derek's back.

Derek was immediately at his throat, humming, and biting.

It sent Justin over the edge.

He bucked against Derek's body, jamming his cock into Derek's fist, pulse after pulse, uttering Derek's name …until he was weeping.

"Shh …" Derek pulled Justin into his arms and clung to him. "You're okay. I'm right here."

And he was.

It was still dark, so Derek wasn't sure what time it was, or why he'd awoken. The weight of Justin's arm draped over him wasn't unusual, but the feel of Justin's lips against the back of his neck was. Justin was lying closer to him than usual. Justin shifted, moved his arm to Derek's waist, and held him in place as he jammed his hard cock up against the small of Derek's back.

That's what woke me up.

Memories of the night before came rushing back—the shower, the living room floor, the kitchen. Justin had been unstoppable. He reached back and placed his hand on Justin's bare ass.

"Justin?"

"Yeah?"

"Nothing." Derek smirked. "I was just making sure it was you."

"Asshole," Justin mumbled against Derek's back, then kissed it.

Derek gained some space and rolled onto his back. He wrapped his hand around the back of Justin's neck and brought him in for a kiss.

"Did you sleep all right?" he asked.

"Never better." Justin ran his hand back and forth across Derek's chest, then down to his stomach, where he played with the thick dark hair that became curlier the further down he traveled.

Derek looked past Justin's body to the bedside table.

"It's four-thirty," he said.

"I hate these early starts." Justin threw his arm across his eyes. "Do I have to get up?"

"Not if I had any say in the matter."

"I have a few minutes." Justin yawned. "I don't have to be at school until six."

"Not until six? Well then. What do you think we should do with all that extra time? A big breakfast? Or maybe you could help me work through the stack of logs that need split."

"I was thinking of something a bit more pleasurable."

"Are you propositioning me, Leary?"

Justin edged closer and whispered, "Perhaps," then used his tongue to play with the lobe of Derek's ear.

Derek groaned, his balls tingling in anticipation of Justin's rough, calloused hands exploring his body. Hands that knew precisely what they were doing. Hands that had without question become familiar with men's bodies—bodies other than his own.

He scrubbed his hand through Justin's hair, and applied pressure, encouraging Justin to continue licking a path from his throat, down to the base of his cock.

Whomever Justin had been with in the past didn't matter.

It really doesn't.

Derek touched the side of Justin's face until Justin looked up. There was a brief silent exchange between them. Something had shifted in Justin last night as if overcoming Nick's voice had freed him somehow. Justin was showing him a sexually aggressive streak, one he hadn't expected would run through Justin's innocent, light-hearted personality.

He arched his back and clung to the bedding. Justin had, after a moment of pause, taken the head of his cock into his mouth, his tongue licking circles around the slit.

Justin took the full length into his throat, gagging, then sucking and stroking it with his tongue, until Derek was close to cumming.

Not yet.

He tapped Justin's shoulder until Justin glanced up at him. The carnal need residing in Justin's eyes was unmistakable. Justin wanted more ...and would readily give more as well.

Justin rumbled out a positive response, crawled up the length of Derek's body, and nudged Derek's legs apart, before reaching for the bedside table drawer.

Justin was going to be late for school.

Chapter Nineteen

Derek stood staring at the apartment door for at least ten minutes before he ventured to slip the key into the lock. Finding the courage to turn the key, would require the support of the person clattering up the stairs, ten minutes late. He looked back over his shoulder.

"Hey, thanks for coming, Bree."

"I couldn't let you do this on your own." Breanne held her hand up. "Yes, I'm well aware. I left you to deal with far worse than this on your own."

"I wasn't going to say anything."

"Oh …" Breanne placed her hand on her hip and pushed past Derek. "Let me do this." She turned the key. The tumbler of the lock thudded open, indifferent and hollow.

Derek reached for the frame of the door as Breanne opened it.

His stomach rolled.

"Whoa—whoa." Breanne nudged her way against Derek's body and slung his arm around her shoulders. "Please don't pass out on me. You're probably more than twice my weight."

"Let me sit for a second."

Derek reached for the nearest wall and slid down to sit on the floor. He stared up at the twelve-foot ceiling. From where he was positioned, he could see all the steel girders of the converted warehouse space, including the one with a band of worn paint one inch wide.

He shut his eyes.

He wasn't sure he was strong enough to move away from that wall. The image of his stepladder tipped on its side, and

Maureen suspended four feet above the floor, was as vivid as the day he'd found her.

Fuck.

His eyes snapped open. Maureen's image at the end of that rope had been replaced. An image of Justin hung in her place. He'd let both of them down.

And then there's your mother.

Do you want me to take a look around?" Breanne asked. "Make sure there's nothing left."

"There shouldn't be much." Derek rose to his feet. "Can you check Maureen's room for me?"

"Sure thing, hun."

Derek walked over to one of the large windows, opened it, and looked down at the busy street below. He'd headed out of town for a few days on business, and Bree had been scheduled to work double shifts at the hospital. They'd agreed Maureen would be fine for a few days on her own. They couldn't have been more wrong.

"There's a full closet of Maureen's drag stuff in here," Breanne called out. "What do you want to do with all of it?"

He'd known the outfits were in there, but he hadn't been ready to make any decisions about them when he'd moved out.

"I have no idea." Derek stepped up behind Breanne and lifted a pink sequined sleeve. Maureen had last worn it at a Valentine's Day drag competition some fifteen years back. He smiled. Maureen's rendition of Valerie Wellington's *A Fool for You* had been divine. He'd watched the video with Maureen many times. "Maybe we can donate everything to Showgirlz."

"That's a great idea," Breanne agreed. "I'll give the club a call tomorrow."

Derek released the sleeve. "Maureen would have wanted them passed on." He followed Breanne to the main living space and then veered off toward the kitchen.

The stainless steel appliances and marble countertops were

part of the reason his apartment was being listed as a *high-end downtown condo* by his realtor. The reclaimed floors and exposed brick feature walls were selling features as well. A renovation that had taken him months to complete. He looked around the expansive space. His hard work had paid off. The only things left to do, schedule some cleaners and hire a staging decorator.

The sale of the apartment would more than pay off the debts accumulated by their company.

Derek flipped open a cupboard in the kitchen. He'd deliberately left Maureen's favorite teacup behind, unable to touch it. If he left it there now, the cleaners would throw it away. It needed to come home with him. Seven years on its own was seven years too long.

"Is that everything?" Breanne asked while eyeing the cup grasped tight in Derek's hand.

"Yeah, but I'd like to stick around for a bit."

"Sure." Breanne juggled the armload of costumes hanging across one arm. She reached out and touched Derek's hand. "If you need me to come back, call me, okay?"

"I'll be fine. And thanks. I appreciate this."

"Any time. I have a lot of making up to do." She squeezed Derek's hand and then took off down the stairs, not quite making it through the building's front doors before releasing a string of obscenities. It sounded like some of the clothing had escaped her grasp.

Derek closed the apartment door behind him and retook his position seated on the floor. A cold breeze rushed through the open window, chilling his skin.

It was a poignant reminder of the cold air that had rushed over his boots, before he'd opened the door, and found Maureen hanging from the girder.

She'd opened all the windows for some reason.

And filled her deceased cat's dish with water and food.

When he'd moved into the building, the resident across the

hall, Maureen, had introduced himself as Maurice, a man in his mid-sixties.

Derek had been pleasant, but never took much notice of eccentric, oddly dressed, elderly man. The polite but impersonal nods and murmurs of acknowledgment changed the day Maurice was taken away in an ambulance.

He'd asked Derek to take care of his cat, Trixie.

Derek grinned.

That damn cat.

Trixie had settled into his place right away, which hadn't been the intended arrangement, but leaving her in Maurice's apartment was out of the question. The rest of the neighbors on the floor had come hammering on his door as soon as he'd arrived home from work.

Apparently, according to many of the neighbors, Trixie had lain on the floor of Maurice's apartment and put her little face against the opening at the bottom of the door, and she hadn't stopped meowing at the top of her lungs since he'd left that morning after feeding her.

At the risk of the homeowners association coming down on his head, or Maurice's, Derek had brought Trixie to stay at his place. He wasn't around for most of the day, but she seemed content in knowing he would return each evening. There had been no further complaints.

Of course, within the first day, she'd managed to leave scratches on every piece of leather furniture he owned. Plus, she'd trashed most of his plants. It had been a rocky start, but she'd grown on him during the ten days Maurice had been in the hospital.

When Maurice returned home, in thanks for watching his cat, he'd invited Derek to come over for some tea and a special white chocolate, cranberry, and cream cheesecake he'd made for him.

After that, Derek had become a regular visitor over at

Maurice's apartment. He made sure his schedule was always free Wednesday evening. Sometimes for tea and cake. Sometimes dinner. And sometimes popcorn and Netflix. Whatever Maurice felt his body was capable of handling.

Maurice had aged well beyond his years, he was lonely, and he was dying. The latter was something Maurice had revealed to Derek on their second meeting. Stage IV lung cancer. He'd stopped treatment a few months before they'd met.

By the third Wednesday, Derek met *Maureen*. Not that he was surprised Maureen existed within Maurice. The colorful boas hanging lazily from every perch-able location, and a bathroom piled high in stage makeup, had Derek wondering if he was ever going to meet her.

Derek looked down at the familiar teacup and traced his finger around the rim. *Cream first, two sugar, and as hot as your ass*. He laughed while setting the cup on the floor beside him. Maureen had never held back on the bawdy compliments where his body was concerned.

His eyes filled with tears.

When Maureen's cancer progressed to the point she was unable to care for herself, he'd taken her in, setting her up in his second bedroom. Maurice had been left behind in the dust of the old apartment in preference to living out her days as Maureen. She'd wanted to go out with a bang of glamor, boas, and sequins, with the tail end of a show tune still perched upon her lips.

Her words.

Derek rubbed his hands on the knees of his pants. Despite the coolness of the room, his palms had become clammy. Once he'd moved Maureen into his place, he'd contacted Breanne, and she'd agreed to check in on Maureen each day before her shift at the hospital began. It made sense. She was a registered nurse. He'd needed her help. And she'd agreed not to tell anyone. Why he'd asked her to do that, keep Maureen a secret, was a mystery he was still trying to unravel.

Within a month of her moving in, Maureen's cat, Trixie, died.

And everything unraveled from there.

Derek touched the cup again. The first time Maureen had tried to commit suicide, he'd found her in the tub, wrists slit, all decked out in an ill-fitting green and yellow sequined dress, and a mess of haphazard makeup.

He'd called 9-1-1, which led to the cruel repugnant treatment that still filled him with regret. He should have said something. He was there as Maureen's advocate, and he'd stood at her bedside in silence.

He scrubbed a hand up through his hair. And Justin. He'd let Justin down by *not* taking him to the hospital. He'd driven him home instead because he was scared of finding himself in the same situation. Scared about how Justin would be treated by emergency staff. Scared that he wouldn't have the balls to stand up for him.

Justin had almost died because of his cowardice.

He didn't deserve him.

He didn't deserve anyone. He'd even let his mother down.

Derek covered his ears with his hands. The sound of his mother sobbing at the other end of the phone still tormented him. His stepfather had left her, and at the time, he hadn't understood why his mother was upset about him abandoning her.

Every day of his life, he'd witnessed that grotesque man beat her. He'd thought his mother would realize she was better off without him, so he hadn't given her the support she needed. He'd never considered for a moment that his mom may have loved her husband.

Two days later, she'd crossed the centerline on the highway, drunk, and with a mission. Derek had found the suicide note addressed to him, propped up against a vodka bottle on her television.

She was killed on impact, but she wasn't the only death on

that stretch of road that night. She'd taken an entire family with her.

Derek scrambled to his feet, slammed the door behind him, and took off down the stairs.

He couldn't pull Justin any further into his life. He'd let him down, and he'd lied to him. He should never have kept Maureen and what happened to his mom a secret. Justin trusted him and he shouldn't. He didn't deserve that trust. He'd deceived the man he loved, and there was no excuse for that. Justin deserved better than what he could offer. It was time to back away.

The first signs of spring were beginning to warm the air, but not enough to keep Justin from turning up the collar of his coat before stepping outside. He'd been visiting his mother at the care home his dad and sister had chosen for her. *Spring Valley Care Center* sounded nicer than it was but not as bad as many of the facilities he'd seen while tagging along with Breanne in her search.

"Justin?"

Justin turned back to see who'd called out to him.

"Melanie!" Justin rolled his collar down and jogged the short distance back into the main entrance area. He grasped her shoulders. "What are you doing here?"

"Visiting my grandma. You?" Melanie replied.

"No, my mom …"

Justin released Melanie and rubbed the back of his neck. He was never going to feel comfortable breaking the news to people about his mom. Somewhere, in the back of his mind, he still hoped her diagnosis was wrong. That with some new medication, she'd be back to normal.

"Oh, no." Melanie grasped Justin's arm. "What happened?"

"Alzheimer's."

"That's horrible. I love your mom."

Justin tipped his head, smiling. "Yeah, she was pretty fond of you as well. I think she was more upset when you moved away than I was."

Melanie pushed Justin's shoulder. "Stop. That's not true."

"Yeah, I know." Justin studied Melanie's face. She was as beautiful as the day she'd waved to him from the back window of her parents' car, bound for the east coast. He hadn't thought he'd ever see her again. "What brings you back to this side of the country? Your grandma?"

"No." Melanie clapped her hands together. "I've moved back."

Justin took a step back, both physically and emotionally.

"Oh good. Great." He crossed his arms, praying she wouldn't ask the question he sensed balanced upon her lips. He hadn't seen a wedding ring on her finger, so he was relatively certain the next thing she'd ask was—

"So, are you married?"

Justin smirked as he attempted to look nonchalant about the whole thing, pretending marriage was the furthest thing from his mind out of choice.

"No. Still single."

"Me too. Now. Divorced two years ago."

He saw the excitement building in Melanie's eyes and the wheels turning behind them. A year ago, before that camping trip, he would've been excited about seeing her again—and discovering she was single. She was the only girl who'd succeeded in redirecting his attention away from Derek, but she was a year too late. His life had changed immensely since then.

"Are you seeing anyone?" she asked.

"Um, yeah." Justin looked off into the distance. This was not the place to tell his ex-girlfriend, the one he'd proposed marriage to in sophomore year at high school, that he was seeing Derek.

"Is it serious? How long have you been together?"

"Together? That's a tricky one. Serious? Yeah."

Melanie gripped her arm, rubbing her elbow through her coat. "That's good to hear." She cocked her head to one side.

"She's a lucky girl. Do I know her?"

"No, you wouldn't."

"Well, let's exchange numbers. We can all three of us meet up for dinner sometime."

Justin hesitated. He couldn't say no because then he'd have to explain himself. He handed Melanie his phone, took hers, and added his name and number to her contacts.

"Do you still hang out with Derek?"

"Yeah," Justin said, and then cleared his throat as beads of perspiration began a slow trickle down the side of his body. The new direction of their conversation was making him uncomfortable, and his body was refusing to cooperate with his attempt to avoid triggering Melanie's inquisitive nature further.

"We started a business together a few years after high school. Renovation and construction. Not now though. I'm doing a culinary course. Derek and I, we split up ...not split up—split up. We're still friends. We just don't work together anymore."

He sucked in a breath, his body vibrating.

"Wow, okay. I'm glad you're still friends. Did he ever find a guy to settle down with, or is he still rampaging his way through the entire gay community."

"I don't know ...we don't talk about that kind of thing. There might be someone, but I could be wrong. He spends a lot of time working, so maybe not. I've never seen anyone—"

Shut up, Justin!

Justin looked away toward the end of the hallway.

"Are you all right?" Melanie touched Justin's arm, catching his attention.

"I'm fine." Justin shook his head. "Visiting with my mom always upsets me."

Sure, blame your mom.

"I can imagine. Hey, is it all right with you if I visit your mom when I'm here seeing my grandma?"

"Sure, but she might not recognize you."

Melanie smiled. "My grandma doesn't either, but she enjoys our visits regardless."

"Then that would be great. Thank you." Justin flipped his collar back up. "I have to head home. Tucker needs his dinner."

"Oh, my God," Melanie shrieked and covered her mouth. "Is he still around? I love Tucker."

"Yeah, the old guy is still around. And still as curious as ever."

Melanie bounced up onto her tiptoes. "I miss him."

Justin beamed, remembering how he and Melanie had spent hours at the park, pitching a ball for Tucker. He'd only been a puppy at the time, but there was a chance he'd remember her.

He and Melanie had enjoyed a fantastic few years together, but when he'd proposed, Melanie had turned him down. Not because she didn't want to marry him, but because her family was moving away, and neither of them had been ready to make it on their own without their parents.

So they'd parted ways. They'd written back and forth for over a year, but the frequency of the letters eventually tapered off, then their correspondence stopped altogether.

"I really do have to go." Justin pointed toward the door. "It was great running into you."

"You too."

Justin slipped into his car and sat there for a moment.

What are the chances?

It was great seeing her again.

He started the car and headed for Derek's. Spaghetti Bolognese was on the menu tonight. And he was starving.

The sunlight was fading into darkness, its final rays reflecting off Derek's truck parked out front. Justin stepped into Derek's house, expecting to see him mulling around, but the house was dark and empty. There was only one other place he could be.

Justin grabbed a warmer coat and headed toward their

makeshift creekside retreat. He was surprised to see a collection of empty beer cans littering the brush beside the decking.

Derek was attempting to keep himself balanced on one of the broken chairs. It was apparent that Derek was drunk.

"Did you drink all these?" Justin counted eight cans in the brush and one in Derek's hand. Far more than he'd ever seen Derek drink before. "What happened?"

Justin sat in the chair next to Derek and reached for his hand, but Derek jerked it out of reach.

"Derek—"

"Nothing." Derek crumpled the can in his hand and pitched it into the brush, then cracked open another. "Everything is fine. Everything is as it should be."

"What the hell does that mean?"

"Nothing."

Justin swore beneath his breath and grabbed a beer for himself. He knew better than to push Derek. If Derek didn't want to talk about something, there was little chance of pulling the information from him.

"Guess who I ran into today?" Justin asked.

"I don't know." Derek dispensed with another can. "Santa Claus?"

"Fuck off." Justin wrapped his arms across his chest. Derek was refusing to make eye contact with him. "Derek—"

"Fine." Derek looked over and stared at Justin, his eyes were bloodshot. "Who?"

"Melanie. She moved back recently."

"Good for her." Derek returned to downing the beer in his hand.

Justin slammed his can down on the deck. "What the hell is going on?"

"Nothing."

This time he grabbed Derek's arm. "Something is bothering you. Tell me what it is."

"Not going to happen."

"Fine. I can see you're doing a great job of handling it on your own." Justin scanned the surrounding area. "Where's Tucker?"

"He's at your house. Your guitar is too."

"Why? Why is he at my house? And my guitar? What's going on?"

Derek rose to his feet. "You've been living at my place for weeks."

"So? That's what we agreed on."

"I changed my mind. I don't want you there anymore."

Justin burst to his feet, chucking the half-empty beer can at Derek. "Where the fuck is this coming from? What changed between this morning and now?"

Derek leaned forward, almost tipping out of his chair as he rummaged through the now empty cooler. "Fuck," he whispered, then looked up toward his house. "I need more beer."

"No, you don't. You need to tell me why you're pitching me out. I deserve to know."

"The only thing you need to know is ...go fuck yourself."

"No." Justin stabbed his finger at Derek's face. "*You* can go fuck yourself!"

Justin took off up the hill toward his house, fighting to keep from slipping on the wet leaves. He could barely see where he was going. The sting of tears had come on fast once he'd turned away from Derek.

What the hell just happened?

Why did he kick me out ...with no explanation?

He clung to a tree as he tried to control the gasping breaths he was taking. They'd awoken in Derek's bed this morning, same as usual. They'd made love as they often did upon waking. Derek had been beneath him, gasping ...sighing, whispering his name.

Telling him how much he loved him.

What changed?

Did I do something wrong?

Justin sat down next to the tree he'd been clinging to and scrolled through the contacts on his phone. He needed to talk to someone. His brother, Adam, would have been his first choice, even though sharing his anguish with his brother would have meant *outing* himself, but it wouldn't have mattered. His brother would have accepted him without question.

And so will Breanne.

It was time he told his big sister everything.

Chapter Twenty

The sun peered through the cloud cover, illuminating the polished tombstones. Breanne was standing at Adam's grave. She'd set a bouquet of Easter lilies atop the stone, and was standing with her arms crossed, with the exception of catching the occasional tear with a damp tissue.

"Hey, sis." Justin wrapped his arms around Breanne and pulled her in for a hug. "Sometimes I feel like he's still with us. That at any moment he's going to run up behind me and tackle me."

"Mom used to get so mad at you two for racing around the house. It's a wonder you didn't break more stuff." She touched Justin's face. "I'm so sorry I wasn't here for his funeral. I just couldn't."

"Don't apologize. I figured you'd had your reasons."

"Thanks, little bro." Breanne motioned to a marble bench a few steps away. "Why did you want to meet here? You sounded upset when you phoned me last night. "

"I wanted the three of us to be together."

Breanne laid her hand on Justin's leg. "Now you're scaring me."

"I'm not dying or anything."

"Then what is going on?"

Justin looked down at the grass beneath his feet, preparing himself. Revealing his tightly held secret was going to be hard. Coming out to friends was difficult enough, but friends were friends. If they decided to drop you as a friend because you were queer, then good riddance.

Family though ...family would leave a massive hole in your

heart if they didn't accept you. There was always a chance he was wrong about his sister.

"The reason I was so upset last night," he said, "is because Derek broke things off with me. Or at least I think he did. He was drunk. I tried to phone him today, but he's not picking up."

"Okay, I'm missing some crucial information here."

"Derek and I, we ..." Justin stared up toward the sky. "We've been seeing each other."

"Of course, you *see* him. You're best friends."

Justin turned to face Breanne. "Please don't make me spell it out, Bree."

Breanne furrowed her brow, and then her eyes opened wide. "Oh! *Seeing*—seeing each other."

"Yeah." Justin scrubbed his face with both hands in an attempt to calm himself. There was so much more to tell Breanne. His relationship with Derek was the easy part.

"I had no idea." She reached for Justin's hand and held it tight. "I mean, I've known Derek was in love with you for years, but—"

Justin ripped his hand away. "You knew? You knew, and you didn't tell me!"

"Derek asked me not to. Plus, neither of us thought you'd be open to shifting your relationship into some kind of *gay for you* situation."

What?

"How could both of you be so sure I wouldn't be interested?"

"We weren't ...we just—"

"You just assumed I wouldn't be. That's what you did."

"He was scared of losing you. Give him a break."

Gay for you?

What a load of...

"For the record, I'm not a *gay for you* kinda guy." Justin exhaled a short laugh. "Derek isn't the only guy I've ever slept with, Bree."

"Oh, I …um." Breanne tugged on the lobe of her ear. "I had no idea. I always thought." She smoothed the fabric of her skirt with both hands. "With all the girls you've dated and everything."

"That's a whole other side of things."

"I don't understand."

Justin shut his eyes and sighed.

"Can we please not talk about my sexual attractions right now?"

"I'm sorry." Breanne put her arm around Justin's shoulders. "So, what happened last night?"

"I came home to his place, same as usual, but he wasn't there. He was at the creek working his way through an entire case of beer."

Justin clenched and unclenched his jaw. "He never drinks that much."

"Did you ask him what was going on?"

"He refused to answer me. He kicked me out and told me to go fuck myself. He'd already dumped Tucker, my guitar, my clothes, everything, back at my house."

"You've been living with him?"

"For the past few weeks." Justin exhaled, fighting to control his emotions from overrunning his ability to speak. "I don't know what happened. Yesterday, before I left for school, he locked me in a kiss that almost brought me to my knees. He told me how much he loved me."

Justin held his forehead in his hand. "Then I come home, and he can't stand the sight of me."

Breanne set her hands in her lap. "I think I might know what happened."

"What? Why?"

"I was with him yesterday. I helped him clear out his apartment."

Justin straightened up. "What? I thought he sold that place years ago."

"No." Breanne shook her head. "He's held on to it. He wasn't ready to part with it, but with the business not doing well, he's decided to sell it so that he can pay off the debts."

Justin leaned forward, hands clasped, his arms atop his legs for support.

"I didn't know any of this. The apartment or the extent of trouble the business is in."

"Derek has a habit of taking on too much. You know that." Breanne brushed a loose strand of hair behind her ear. "Blames himself for far too much."

"That doesn't explain why he chased me off last night." Justin peered over at Breanne. "And it doesn't explain why you know more about this than I do."

Breanne shrugged. "I have no idea why he confides in me."

"So, what happened yesterday?" Justin asked.

"It's not so much what happened yesterday." Breanne sighed. "It's what happened in that apartment seven years ago." She held Justin's hand. "Do you remember Maurice?"

"Across the hall? Yeah. Went by Maureen most of the time, right?"

"That's the one." Breanne pursed her lips. "Did Derek tell you about Maureen's cancer?"

"No." Justin's nostrils flared. "He did not."

"For fuck's sake, Derek," Breanne whispered.

"Maureen had lung cancer," she said. "When she started having difficulty caring for herself, Derek took her in. He set her up in the second bedroom."

He what?

Fucking asshole. That's why Derek never wanted me to come by his apartment. All this time I thought he was keeping a boy-toy tied up over there.

Fuck.

"Great. Thanks, guys. Keep me in the dark like a fucking irrelevant mushroom." Justin rose to his feet. "What happened seven years ago that everyone, except me, knows about?"

"It's not like that."

"Yes, it is. It's exactly like that." He crossed his arms. "Tell me what happened."

"Maureen, she was suffering emotionally. When her cat passed away, she didn't see the point of carrying on. That damn cat was the only thing keeping Maureen tethered to the living."

She looked up at Justin. "Seven years ago, Derek walked into his apartment and found Maureen hanging from the girders."

Justin sat back down and covered his mouth with his hands.

"Oh, my God. Why didn't he tell me?"

"I don't know." Breanne wiped her face with a tissue and took a deep breath. "I assumed he would. I thought for sure he would confide in you." She turned away from Justin, her body trembling. "I abandoned him. I was weak ...and I took off."

"That's why you moved away," Justin whispered to Breanne as he used his thumb to wipe a tear from her cheek. "Is there anything else Derek hasn't told me?"

"Did he tell you what happened to his mom?"

"No." Justin erupted to his feet and strode off across the lawn to the far side of the row of plots, then stormed back. His trust in Derek was disappearing fast. Derek had kept life-altering events secret from him. That meant there could be more secrets Derek hadn't even told Breanne.

With that revelation, his trust in Derek evaporated.

"Do you want to know about his mom?" Breanne asked.

Justin lowered himself onto the bench beside her. "No."

"I'm sorry." Breanne set her hand on Justin's back. "I had no idea he was keeping so much from you." She laid her head on Justin's shoulder

"It doesn't matter anymore," Justin said. "He and I are done."

He was enjoying the moment of silence with his sister, but he'd brought her here for more than a discussion about his relationship problems with Derek.

"Bree," Justin said, but his voice came out sounding hoarse, forced.

Deep breath, Justin.

"I was raped last spring."

Breanne pulled away. Both hands flew to her throat, her eyes unblinking.

She didn't speak.

"We were camping, and I ended up in another guy's tent …Sam's cousin. He was in town." Justin stopped to catch his breath. "Long story as to why I was there, but I was. We started fooling around, which I would normally have reservations about, being that he was Sam's cousin and all, but I was drunk. So …yeah."

Breanne covered her mouth, tears soaking her cheeks.

Still silent.

"He turned on me." Justin's chin quivered, despite his efforts to stop it as tears created a path to his lips. "He held me down and raped me."

"Oh, Justin." Breanne reached for him and pulled him into a hug. "I am so sorry."

Justin licked the salty tears from his lips as he sunk further into his sister's embrace. He was exhausted. The rest of what happened that night would need to be shared another time.

Derek finished unloading the equipment needed to refinish the flooring in the heritage Tudor he'd taken on. He looked back before closing the door.

Justin was standing at the base of the front steps, work clothes on as if ready to start the job.

"What the hell are you doing here?" Derek asked.

"I promised you I'd help with this job, so I'm here to help."

"That was over a month ago."

"So?" Justin shifted his weight over to one foot and tucked his thumb into his tool belt. "I don't break my promises. You know that."

Derek stormed away from the front entry as Justin stepped inside.

"I don't want you here," he said.

"Tough, I'm here. There's no way you can finish this job on time without my help." Justin wandered over to the doorway leading into the parlor. "Where do you want me to start?"

Anywhere but here.

He knew Justin wouldn't back down. He'd never known Justin to break a single promise in all the years he'd known him. He should have been expecting him to show up.

Derek knew looking straight into Justin's eyes would be agony, so he did not raise his focus any higher than Justin's shoulders. "Start in the parlor. I'll stay on the opposite side of the house."

"You don't have to be an asshole about this," Justin said. "You broke things off with me, for whatever reason. Sure, it would've been nice if you'd shared that reason with me, but whatever, it's done. I'm here to fulfill my promise to finish this damn job with you."

"Fine, then instead of standing around talking, start."

Justin whispered, "Whatever," beneath his breath and strode off through the parlor doors.

Please make him leave.

Derek had been doing his best to protect himself …and others. Ever since he'd pushed Justin out of his life, he'd sacrificed and alienated everyone he felt a connection with or loved.

Sam, Karen, even Bree …everyone. Karen had been so incredibly hurt when he'd refused her invitation to Brittany's birthday party.

It's for the best.

Having Justin move about the space, knowing every heady scent and intricate contour hidden beneath his clothes, forcing him to remember the sound of Justin's voice in song …and in climax.

Yearning to see Justin's eyes light up when he was excited, amused ...aroused.

His whispering, I love you, in his ear...

Derek almost collapsed, his heart aching to be reunited with Justin's.

He steadied himself against the wall and turned toward the kitchen to find somewhere to sit and attempt to gather his thoughts.

Looking around at the kitchen floor, he decided to start there. The owners had asked him to retain some of the character of the worn, well-traveled hardwood in that space.

Giving this floor specialized treatment, plus working with all the little nooks and crannies, meant it was going to take him longer to complete this small room and attached butlers' pantry than it would take Justin to complete the parlor.

He crouched on the floor to assess the extent of the dirt and grease buildup at the base of the cabinets. He was going to need a sharp putty knife to scrape all the crud away.

As he scraped the edge of the floor where it met the wall, he wished time would pass faster, but it didn't. It seemed to take forever for the hours to pass. Thankfully, Justin wasn't in a singing mood.

An unfamiliar voice rang through the front entry.

"Justin?"

—the sound of Justin's boots leaving the parlor.

"Melanie. What are you doing here?"

"I brought you some lunch. Your dad told me you were working over at the old Miller place."

Derek stepped into the dining room within sight of where Justin and Melanie were standing. "That still doesn't explain what you're doing here."

"Oh, my god! Derek!" Melanie rushed at him and wrapped her arms around his body. He didn't reciprocate. His heart, if it had a voice, would be screaming in agony.

Please, no ...why is she here?

"Melanie," was the extent of speech he was able to manage.

"I was hoping you'd be here," Melanie said. "I guess Justin has told you we're seeing each other again." She clapped her hands together. "Isn't that hilarious after all these years?"

Derek clenched his jaw as he resisted the urge to act on his spiraling emotions. Justin had decided to move on without him.

Of course he did.

You fucking chased him away.

"Remember, I told you I bumped into Melanie a few weeks back," Justin said. "I decided to give her a call when my previous relationship fell apart unexpectedly."

Crushing despair was threatening to tear Derek open. Tear him open and expose the irrational fear that was keeping him from falling to his knees and begging Justin to take him back.

He was trembling, unable to speak, so he turned back toward the kitchen in silence.

"What's wrong with Derek?" he heard Melanie ask Justin.

He didn't hear Justin's response.

There was a quiet conversation about heading to a local park to eat lunch. Then it was quiet.

When Derek heard the door close behind them, he sunk to his knees in tears.

Why are you doing this to me?

He grabbed ahold of the putty knife and pitched it across the room. It skittered to a stop at the far side of the living room, irrelevant, and soon to be forgotten.

Derek stumbled to his feet and careened across the room, using the walls to support himself, then the hollering and screaming started. Guttural and tormented.

He dropped to his knees.

I can't be here.

I can't be here to watch this.

I just can't...

Derek pulled out his phone and texted his realtor.

He had another property he needed to sell. It wasn't completely renovated yet, but the house sat on a secluded piece of acreage with a creek nearby.

Chapter Twenty One

The door of the storage container slammed closed. It sounded as empty as Derek felt. The trucking company transporting his belongings to his new house would be there in the morning.

He took a moment to take a last look around. He had once loved this house nestled within stands of immense cedars and spruce, a house he'd bought so he'd have a reason to spend more time with Justin. Now he wanted nothing more to do with the place. Every surface of that house had been touched by Justin at some point during their renovation.

During the few weeks Justin had been living with him, cooking with him in the kitchen, working on the deck together, hanging out in the living room watching movies and playing video games, and laughing their asses off for no apparent reason, had seemed destined.

And the shower, the shower they'd made love in countless times. The shower Justin had first trusted him with his body in. The glass, the tiles, even the scent of the soap. Everything took him right back. The feel of Justin's hands turning him to face the corner of the shower stall. Justin's heavy breath heating the back of his neck as he filled him, time and time again, groaning and sighing—biting his shoulder as he came.

Derek's face flushed, the vein at his temple pulsing. The metal of the storage container was unforgiving as Derek propelled his fist into it. A life with Justin was the only thing he'd ever wanted, and he'd ruined it by lying to him. He'd pushed the only man he ever loved away because he knew he'd let Justin down again. And he'd been cruel about it, the way he'd chased Justin out of his life. He'd taken Justin's love for him and thrown it back in his face.

It was time for him to move on. Maybe Melanie could provide Justin with the love and honesty he deserved. Justin had so much love to give. He deserved to be happy.

He'd told Karen he wasn't moving until next week to avoid goodbyes. They rarely spoke anymore, but he knew she'd throw some kind of farewell party, and she'd expect Justin to be in attendance. There was little chance Justin would show up, but if he did, it would be awkward. Karen would know something was up, and citing their recent breakup as the reason he was moving away wasn't a conversation he wanted to have with her. They'd never told anyone of their brief love affair. They'd wanted to keep it to themselves for a while. To enjoy the hushed whispers and looks between them when amongst friends, the tension of their secret exciting their desire.

He looked toward the path that led to Justin's house. He needed to catch a glimpse of Justin one last time before he left. It was a warm evening, and he knew Justin had a few people over. Most of the guests would be out on the patio. There was a decent chance Justin would be out there with them.

A reluctant smile graced his face as Tucker came racing along the path, tail wagging. Derek was going to miss the dog's regular appearances at his screen door, looking for treats. He'd left a note for the new homeowners, telling them about Tucker, and where the dog lived.

He ruffled the fur of Tucker's shaggy head. It was going to be confusing for him to arrive at that screen door to find people he didn't know inside. People he hadn't known from the time he was a puppy. Derek could still remember the scent of Tucker's puppy head.

He wiped a stream of tears off his cheek with his forearm as he squatted to scratch Tucker's ears. He pressed his forehead to Tucker's. He was the only friend he had left.

And he had to leave him behind.

Tucker gave his face a good licking and then ran off toward Justin's house.

Following behind at a slower pace, Derek reminisced about the many times he'd been through and beneath these trees, his heart quickening each time he approached Justin's house, knowing Justin was waiting for him, regardless of what they'd planned. As long as Justin was with him.

Derek heard the music before he saw the faint glow emanating from Justin's patio lights through the trees. The sound of people talking and laughing almost made him turn back.

He stuffed his hands into his pockets as a shiver ran up his spine. There were people he'd never met milling around in a home he and Justin had built together. It felt wrong.

Derek clenched his jaw. Justin had stepped out onto the patio, his smile warm but reserved as he circulated amongst the guests. Justin lit a cigarette, leaned against a railing enclosing the patio, and peered out into the darkness. The position of the patio lights and distinct angle of Justin's jaw cast a moving display of light and shade against the shoulder of his shirt.

Justin stopped scanning the surround and concentrated on one spot.

His spot.

"I'll never stop loving you," Derek whispered, then turned away.

The driveway seemed shorter than usual. It spilled out onto the road before Derek had a chance to process the way Justin had been looking at him from the patio.

There had been sorrow there. Deep, painful sadness clouding Justin's expression.

I did that to him.

Months had passed since they'd completed the flooring job. And despite the words Justin had spoken on that first day about their breakup being in the past, Justin had shown up for work each day, his eyes conveying a glimmer of hope. As if he was waiting for Derek to change his mind.

Derek slowed his truck down and pulled over onto the shoulder of the road. He lowered his forehead to rest on the steering wheel.

What are you so damned afraid of, Derek?

Justin had asked him that same question the day they'd dropped their defenses. The day their love for one another had merged with the heat of their physical attraction. And ignited.

An ignition and fire that could have been lit so many times over the years.

He closed his eyes as the memory of their first camping trip slipped into his mind.

The surrounding area was pitch black, mocking the attempt of their camping lantern to provide any proper light. Derek and Justin stumbled into their tent, laughing, and crawled in the direction of their sleeping bags, and wriggled into them.

Once Derek was settled in, he turned to face Justin.

Justin's face was a hair's breadth from his own.

Unmoving, they stared at each other for what seemed an eternity to Derek, their breath mingling and creating a heated space between them.

Derek licked his lips, imagining the feel and taste of Justin's on his own. When Justin blinked but didn't look away, his heart fluttered with yearning. If he stayed even a moment longer with Justin's lips so close to his own, there would be no stopping him from capturing them.

He rolled over, breaking the odd standoff they appeared to have been having.

As the sun crested the tree line, creating shimmering beams of light that cut straight through the thin fabric of the tent, Derek awoke beneath the weight of Justin's arm draped over him.

Justin shifted behind him.

Derek closed his eyes as he mumbled, "Please," under his

breath, and leaned back against Justin's body, but Justin didn't respond to his subtle advance.

He'd been insane to think Justin was gay.

Or that he'd be the least bit interested in him if he were.

"Damn it's cold," Derek said as he hauled his sleeping bag further up onto his shoulders, forcing Justin to lift his arm away.

He tucked his arm against his chest. His cheeks heated despite the cold as he chastised himself for considering the possibility that Justin had been okay with the closeness of their bodies. That Justin had been trying to initiate something.

Derek gripped the steering wheel as he straightened up. It had been too soon in their relationship. They'd barely known each other. Their feelings had needed time to grow and mature. Except by the time a solid bond had formed between them, a pattern of denial had set in.

Justin had been right all those months back. They'd been a couple, a couple in love for years and hadn't even realized it. And he'd broken off their commitment to one another as if they'd only been together a few weeks.

Justin deserves an explanation.

Derek looked down at his phone. It was tempting, but phoning Justin would be the coward's way out. Texting him would be even worse. He turned the truck around, headed back the way he came, and pulled into Justin's driveway.

The perimeter of Justin's circular driveway was packed with vehicles. Derek eased past them and stopped in a space facing Justin's house. He needed to make a decision. Go inside and face the awkwardness of running into people he knew. Or call Justin and ask him to come out.

He looked at his phone again but tossed it to one side when a large group of people walked past his truck. There were too many people around.

Derek took a moment to clear his head. Maybe it was better

if he left without speaking to him. He'd caused him enough pain.

He backed up, then popped the truck into drive.

It was time to start clean.

The deafening, reverberating sound of someone pounding on the side of his truck had him slamming on the brakes.

Justin excused himself and strode toward the spot where he'd seen Derek standing. The ferns were trampled, but there was no sight of him, so he headed off down the path that connected their two properties. By the time he arrived at Derek's house, he was nowhere in sight.

His truck was gone. And so were the contents of his house.

Peering into the blackness beyond the windows and realizing the finality of the emptiness, Justin panicked and hammered frantically on the windows.

He raced around to the back of the house in case the door was unlocked.

Please be here.

The handle of the door refused to turn. Justin pressed his back against it and sunk to the ground, his mind racing through scenarios where Derek might be back any minute.

He knew he was lying to himself.

Derek wasn't coming back. The only remnants of the man he'd spent every waking moment with for almost twenty years, had been reduced to a steel box in his driveway.

You weren't supposed to have left yet.

He had intended to wander over to Derek's over the next few days. See him one last time before he moved away to the reclusive cabin he'd bought in the wooded area of Lancaster, nearly ten hours away. There was little chance Derek would be back this way again.

Justin pounded on the container, then headed back toward the trail. He needed to see Derek. If he had to drive after him and chase him down, he would.

He needed to tell Derek he was still in love with him—that he'd never stop loving him.

That no one would ever be able to replace what they had.

Not ever.

He started running, tears streaking down his face, his unsteady feet tripping over every exposed root crossing his path. Derek had left, and not even said goodbye to him.

How could you do this to me?

Justin picked up speed, changing direction to save time. He needed to find his keys and be on the road before Derek put too much distance between them. His little car was no match for the power of Derek's truck. He needed to catch up before Derek hit the main highway out of town.

As Justin emerged at the edge of his property, he spotted the familiar black pickup parked in his driveway through the trees. When the reversing lights came on, and the wheels turned to drive away, Justin fought his way through a grove of huckleberry bushes at the edge of his driveway, and pushed a group of his guests out of his way, to reach Derek before he drove off.

Stop. Goddamn it, Derek. Stop.

Justin hammered on the back panel of the truck, and then the driver's side window until Derek slammed on his brakes. Derek just stared at him through the glass of the window.

Don't do this to me.

"Please," Justin cried as he placed his hands on the window, his face coated in perspiration, tears, and the dust he'd kicked up while racing along the path.

Derek appeared to sigh and motioned for Justin to climb into the passenger seat.

Justin slammed the door after climbing in and stared out through the front windshield in silence as Derek pulled the truck off the driveway onto a patch of wild grass.

"You were going to leave without seeing me." Justin crossed his arms, maintaining his attention on the brush illuminated by the truck's headlights.

"Yeah," Derek peered over at Justin, then stared at the instrument panel on his dash. He switched the engine and headlights off, plunging them into darkness, the only light, the strings of lanterns decorating Justin's front porch. "I came here to explain."

"By lurking at the edge of my yard?"

"No, not then. Now."

"Derek, you were about to drive away." Justin rubbed away a latent tear with the heel of his hand. "Did you even try to find me? Did you go inside? Phone me? Text me?"

Justin took Derek's silence as a no.

"Why did you lie about when you were moving?" he asked. "Because you didn't want to see me?"

"I wanted to see you. I did—"

"Then why were you driving away?"

"I wasn't sure what to do."

"Sticking around and seeing me would have been nice."

Derek looked out through his side window. "I was afraid seeing you would tear my heart out."

"Derek, look at me." Justin shifted in his seat until he was facing Derek. "My heart has been torn from my chest every single day since you told me to fuck off."

Derek sucked in a ragged breath and released the steering wheel he'd been choking. "I never meant to hurt you." He slammed his hands against the dashboard. "Your love has been the only thing I've ever wanted. From the first day we met, I knew I wanted you in my life."

"Dammit, Derek," Justin whispered as the depth of anguish and regret in Derek's eyes began a steady strangulation of his heart. "Why the hell are we doing this to each other?"

Derek managed a shaky, "I don't know."

Justin placed his hand on Derek's face, brushed at the stubble with his thumb, and held Derek's chin to keep him from looking away. "I will *never* stop loving you."

"Please don't say that."

"Why? It's the truth. Neither of us will ever find the kind of love we have between us ever again." Justin settled back in his seat. "I don't understand why you're running."

Derek leaned his head against his headrest and closed his eyes. "When you first told me you were in love with me, my first impulse was to run."

He stopped, and his brow creased. "I'd convinced myself that the assault was the reason I couldn't take that step with you. To admit I was in love with you."

"And when you chased me off?"

Derek looked out through the windshield. "I didn't want to let you down again. You trusted me, and I didn't deserve it. You would have left me eventually."

"So, you decided to leave me before I left you?"

"Something like that."

"God, Derek. You're such an idiot sometimes. You had no right to impose your screwed up assumptions on me."

Justin tapped the toe of his boot against the carpeted wheel-well. "And what do you mean, you don't deserve my trust? What did you do?"

"It doesn't matter."

"Yes, it does."

"No, I need to go. I have a long drive ahead of me."

"Whoa. Hang on." Justin clung to Derek's arm to keep him from restarting the truck. "Did I say something wrong?"

"No. Yes." Derek wiped a rivulet of tears from his chin and ran his hand up into his hair. "Knowing we still love each other is going to make leaving so much worse."

"Then why the hell are you leaving?"

"I have to, Justin."

"Why?" Justin slipped his hand into Derek's and squeezed it. "I've been trying to function without you since we split. And no matter what I do, it isn't working. And I suspect it isn't working for you either." He set his hand on Derek's thigh. "Please tell me why you want to rip us apart."

Derek stared into his lap. "There are parts of my life I've kept secret from you over the years. I would never expect you to forgive me for lying to you."

"Isn't that my decision? Plus, I might know more than you think."

Derek peered over at him. "Bree?"

"Yeah, but you should have told me yourself." Justin settled back in his seat. "I might have been a little pissed off at first, given the amount of time that had passed, but I know what you're like, always trying to protect everyone."

He tapped the console between the seats. "Maurice, your mom ...that family. Even what happened to me. You are not responsible for any of it. You need to stop blaming yourself."

"I can't." Derek covered the side of his face with his hand, then rubbed his knuckles along his jawline. "I don't want to." He glanced over at Justin. "I've done enough damage. I need to go."

Justin blinked a few times and threw the passenger door open.

So, you're going to trample all over my heart some more.

That's not the least bit damaging.

Fuck you.

"You want to punish yourself, go ahead, but leave me out of it." Justin leaped onto the ground. "And by the way, I take back what I said. I'll find some way to get over you. Maybe if I fuck my way through every guy in the whole damn state, I'll forget all about you."

"Justin, that's not—"

Justin slammed the passenger door and strode off toward his house.

I don't want to..., he says.

I've done enough damage..., he says.

"Fucking ridiculous," Justin muttered as he approached the steps to his front porch. He ignored Derek yelling at him to stop.

Piss off.

Justin changed direction, heading toward the woods instead. He didn't want to go into his house with Derek on his ass. No one other than Breanne knew he and Derek had been lovers.

And it was pointless having their friends find out now.

"Justin!"

Justin held his middle finger up above his head as he kept walking. "Fuck off, Derek!"

He was surprised Derek was still following him.

"Justin—"

"I said fuck off."

Maybe fucking his way across the state wasn't such a bad idea. It would certainly keep him occupied. Add a steady stream of alcohol, and he'd be too wrecked to think about Derek.

Maybe I could even make a porn video and send it to him.

Or a whole boxed set.

He almost tripped over a tree root in the darkness. They were moving further from the house, losing any ambient light from it. He'd have to proceed from memory.

Okay ...maybe doing porn is a bit much.

"Justin!"

He spun to face Derek. "What?"

"Can you stop for a second?"

"Why? I thought you were done with the whole *damage* thing." Justin turned from Derek and walked away. "I can't say the same for myself. You keep following me, and you'll be on the receiving end of some damage. It's been almost a year since I broke your nose last."

"You wouldn't—"

Justin spun on Derek. "Try me."

Derek clenched his jaw but left his arms at his sides. "I don't want to fight you."

"Then stop following me. Please, leave me alone." Justin turned his back to Derek and rubbed away a fresh stream of tears from his eyes as he continued walking. "If you're going to leave, please, leave. I can't take any more of this. You're ripping me apart all over again."

He took a deep breath. He loved these woods. They'd spent so much time here together. It was going to be difficult to separate his memory of Derek from them.

The leaves of the aspen trees in the grove fluttered overhead, rustling in the breeze. The only other sound, Derek sobbing behind him.

Don't, Derek. Please.

"I don't know what to do." Derek stared at the ground. "I've fucked everything up."

"Everything? Like what?"

"You went through a lot to heal yourself. I should have been there for you."

"Derek, you *were* there for me. In your weird, roundabout, stalker kind of way. I knew you'd come running if I called you." Justin cocked his head to one side. "So, what else have you been beating yourself up over?"

Derek rubbed his forehead with the palm of his hand. "I should have taken you to the hospital that night. I should have insisted you be checked out."

"I didn't want to go to the hospital, and I wouldn't have let you force me." Justin placed his hand on Derek's shoulder. He'd missed the solid strength of Derek's body.

And the rush of raw power that swept over him as Derek submitted beneath him.

Stop it.

"Anything else?" he asked.

Derek shrugged.

"That's it?" Had Derek almost left him for that? Stubbornness, stupidity, and conversations that should have happened. "You should have talked to me instead of kicking me out. If I'd wanted to leave you after what you've just told me, I would have left on my own."

Justin moved his hand to Derek's chest as he moved closer to Derek's body. He took a few steps forward until Derek's back was pressed up against one of the few cedars in the grove.

He placed his thigh between Derek's legs, against his groin, to keep him from slipping away, and looked up as the cloud cover cleared, and the moonlight cut through the still shivering leaves of the aspen trees, creating a dancing kaleidoscope of light and shadow.

Derek's face came into view as the light changed, his panting breath, uncertain.

So damn gorgeous.

"I would never have left you," Justin whispered as he pulled Derek toward him. He pressed his lips to Derek's, not sure if Derek would even reciprocate.

Please.

Derek hesitated at first, but then the heat and love swept him up. "God, I've missed you," he murmured against Justin's lips, then traveled along the base of Justin's collarbone with his tongue, and sucked his skin, until Justin shuddered and groaned.

Justin dug his fingers into Derek's shoulders.

"I don't want you to go," Justin said, his voice soft, his lips hovering above Derek's before he captured them again.

Derek released him and placed his forehead against Justin's as he stroked the peak of Justin's ears with his thumbs. "Are you sure you want me to stay?"

"Only if we're done playing games." Justin held tight to Derek's hands to keep them from retreating away from his face. "If we're done, I won't let you run again. You'll be stuck with me."

Derek grinned and released a short laugh. "I sold my damn house, Leary."

"So?" Justin slipped his hand from Derek's and caressed the

hardening flesh beneath the zipper of Derek's jeans. "Phone the transport company. Ask them to move the container next door." Derek looked up, his fast beating lashes and creased brow, threatening to collide.

God, you're adorable.

"You want me to move in with you?" Derek asked.

"No, I thought we could erect a tent in the yard for you." Justin brushed his fingers along the edge of Derek's ear, then down to his chin. "We've been heading in this direction since we were sixteen. There's nothing to be afraid of."

Justin pressed his lips to Derek's, a passionate, mind-altering kiss, filled with love, and reconciliation. Derek growled and stripped Justin's shirt off over his head and let it drop to the ground, then pulled Justin's mouth back to join his, ravenous to possess him.

Derek's belt unlatched with the swift movement of Justin's hands, and he ripped Derek's shirt open, the buttons dispersing onto the mossy ground. He kissed and nipped his way down along Derek's jawline until he found the spot on Derek's throat he'd been craving.

The sounds Derek made as he licked and sucked the skin there, were enough to make him hard, even without the added stimulation of Derek's hips undulating against him.

He needed more.

Justin unbuttoned his pants and shifted them off his hips, enough for Derek's hands to make their way past the restrictive waistband. He arched his back as Derek's hand traced a path down along the crease of his ass. "Yes, baby ...please." A single finger ran along his taint.

God, yes.

"Please?" Derek smiled against Justin's throat as he continued teasing him, dragging one finger after another from Justin's balls to the edge of where Justin wanted him to be.

Justin closed his eyes.

It had been far too long. He was aching.

"You and Melanie aren't still together, are you?" The question came out of nowhere, catching Justin off guard. It hadn't even crossed his mind that Derek didn't know.

"No, Melanie and I ...it was over before it started." Justin stroked his fingers through the curls of Derek's hair, his cock begging to be released as Derek continued to torment him.

He set his hand on Derek's arm to stop him. "It wouldn't have been right to let her think we had a future together. I'd never be able to give her the devotion she deserves. My love for you would never allow anyone else in. Not after what we'd shared."

Derek smiled and set a soft kiss on Justin's lips as he swept his hands up from beneath Justin's waistband onto his back. His rough, powerful hands started at Justin's shoulders and then caressed the length of Justin's body until Justin was begging Derek to take him.

He grabbed Justin, pressed his chest against the tree, and hauled Justin's pants down around his ankles. Justin rearranged the placement of his hands to support himself.

Derek's heated breath drifted over his shoulder, his hands caressing Justin's body down his torso, over his hips, and along his thighs. Justin turned his head enough to taste Derek's lips on his again. The world outside disappeared as Derek's arm wrapped around his body.

He felt safe with him.

"Are you sure you want to do this here?" Derek asked, his voice deep, smooth, and raw with hunger. It wasn't really a question. There was no need to answer it.

Derek kissed the back of Justin's neck, accompanied by the sound and shuffle of Derek's jeans and a condom wrapper being ripped open. Derek shifted one of his hands and gripped tight to Justin's hips, keeping Justin in place.

Justin swore beneath his breath as Derek's cock slid up along his spine.

"Are you all right?" Derek asked.

"Yeah." Justin reached back for Derek's leg. There was a brief moment of panic, but it passed before taking hold. Derek would never do anything that might hurt him.

He sighed in response as Derek's lubed finger slid up into his ass—in and out until he began to relax. "I can't believe you still carry all of that stuff around with you," Justin joked.

"Habit." Derek stroked his free hand along Justin's shoulder.

Justin placed his forehead on the bark of the tree. "I need to tell you something."

"Now?"

"It's important." Justin touched Derek's arm. "The day you came to pick me up at the hospital. I told you that lots of guys had claimed my ass." He rested his head back against Derek's shoulder. "It's not true. You're the only one. I said those things to hurt you."

Derek removed his finger, replacing it with the head of his cock. He eased it in, partially, then stopped. "You have no idea how hot that makes me," he whispered. "To know you're mine."

They both took a moment to steady their breathing.

"Always." Justin reached back and tapped Derek on the hip. "Okay ...I'm ready."

"I love you," Derek whispered, then kissed Justin's cheek. There was no need to respond. Derek knew how much he loved him.

Justin tipped his head forward, groaning until the border between pain and pleasure slipped fully into pleasure as Derek gripped tight to his hips and undulated upward.

Derek wrapped his arm around Justin's chest, supporting him—protecting him.

Tears spilled down Justin's cheeks.

His world was right again.

Chapter Twenty Two

"Keep your eyes closed." Derek guided Justin away from his truck, not wanting Justin to stumble down the slight slope. The makeshift blindfold wasn't exactly opaque, but it had proved sufficient in obscuring where he was headed.

As a bonus, driving around in circles through alleyways and back roads, in addition to every street in their neighborhood, had caused Justin to start laughing uncontrollably.

There's no way he knows where we are.

"Are you still okay under there?"

"Yes, but where the hell are we?" Justin gripped tight to Derek's arm when he almost slipped. "And why are we standing outside in the dark? In the middle of a rainstorm?"

"Patience." Derek smirked, but inside his guts were churning. He'd never been as nervous about anything in his life.

Everything is going to be fine.

He had Justin back up until the edge of the bench was behind him. "Okay, sit."

Justin launched himself off the bench, almost bowling Derek over. "It's soaked."

"I don't care. You can change into dry jeans when we're back home. Sit."

"Fine." Justin lowered himself back onto the wet. "This better be good."

Oh, god, I hope so.

"You can take off the blindfold now." Derek stepped back so Justin could take in where they were.

"The school bleachers?" Justin brushed some droplets of rain from his nose. "What are we doing here?"

Derek cleared his throat, the rapid thrum of his pulse almost deafening him. "Remember when we were sitting on these bleachers." He closed his eyes and looked skyward, then back at Justin. "When we were in high school, avoiding the principal's office ...and I asked you a question?"

"Yeah, of course. I regretted not saying yes, from the moment I started laughing."

Justin leaned forward and rubbed his wet hands on his jeans. "Is that why we're here? To replay that moment?"

"Sort of." Derek took a deep breath.

Please don't pass out.

Justin leaned back. "What's going on? You look like you're about to throw up."

"You said that exact thing the day I asked if you were interested in me."

"Well, if you haven't figured out I'm interested in you by now, you need your head examined."

Just do it.

Derek reached into his jacket pocket, and then lowered himself down onto one knee. "I know it's crazy, and I've said it before, but I knew. I knew I wanted to spend my life with you from the first day we met."

"That doesn't sound the least bit crazy to me." Justin cupped Derek's face and set a kiss on his lips, then sat back. "Sorry ...I felt the need to kiss you."

He waved his hand at Derek. "Go ahead."

Derek lowered his head, then looked up at Justin. He opened the box he'd been enveloping in his hand. "Justin, nothing would make me happier than having you by my side as my husband."

He licked his lips, staring at Justin. He'd be devastated if Justin said no.

Far too many seconds ticked by.

Justin blinked. "Oh, you actually want me to answer that." He nudged Derek's shoulder, almost knocking him over, then held out his left hand. "You know damn well what the answer is."

Derek slipped the ring onto Justin's finger, then sunk both knees into the wet mud, and shuffled closer. He held Justin's face for a moment, savoring Justin's smile, then gave him the most earnest, loving, and heated kiss he could manage.

Justin hauled them both to their feet, still locked together, and grinned against Derek's lips.

"What?" Derek asked.

"I was just thinking …are we going to be Lawrence-Learys?" He hauled Derek up the slope toward the truck, snorting with laughter. "Or Leary-Lawrences?"

"Both of them sound like some kind of comedy act."

"Oh …" Justin clapped his hands together. "Good idea. We could tour the world."

Derek grinned and pressed Justin up against the truck. Day by day, his goofy, mischievous lunatic of a best friend was slowly returning to him.

He knew Justin would never be entirely whole again, but over time, he hoped they would learn to weather those stretches of darkness together.

Author's Notes

Quite often when I'm looking for subject matter to write about within the contemporary LGBTQ Romantic Fiction genre, I'll explore areas of the LGBTQ community that readers may know very little about. Sometimes I'll proceed with a book, most times I won't. This is my second book where I tackle a difficult subject. The first being *Simply Marvelous*, where my main character undergoes sexual reassignment surgery for all the wrong reasons.

With *Shadows On My Soul*, during my search for subject matter, I spoke with a friend who had experience with male survivors of sexual assault. During our conversation, they went into detail about the misconceptions surrounding male rape. I then spoke with another friend who worked in victim's services, specifically supporting sexual assault victims, including men. The stories and statistics they shared with me solidified my decision to tell this story. I felt it was important to open a dialogue on some level about the existence of male rape, the journey that male survivors must travel, and how that journey can affect their relationships, romantic or otherwise

At times the writing of this book took a serious toll on me, emotionally, mentally, and physically. I would take lengthy breaks. Sometimes months. Almost two years at one point. Then I would dive back into it and do what I could to battle the depression, the anger, and the tears that came along with using the research I'd gathered to torment Justin, a gentle, fun loving, and carefree soul. There were many times I tried to bury the book, push it to the back of my mind, never to be written, but it kept resurfacing. Justin wanted his story to be told, and with some serious trepidation, I decided to honor that.

Facts and Myths about Male Sexual Assault

About 1 in 25 reported sexual assaults is against a man. As with male sexual violence against women, sexual violence against men is motivated by the desire to dominate and use sex as a weapon against the victim. The majority of the perpetrators of sexual violence against men are white, heterosexual men .

Male victims experience similar effects of sexual violence as female victims such as shame, grief, anger and fear. Male victims may also have issues surrounding their sexual and/or gender identity after a sexual assault. Issues of reporting and talking about their experiences, challenges for all victims of sexual violence, may be especially difficult for male victims because of gender socialization issues.

For our society to acknowledge that men are raped, we must first recognize and acknowledge that men can be vulnerable. Both men and women are socialized to see men as powerful, assertive, and in control of their bodies. It may be challenging for some to think of men being the victims of sexual crimes because it is challenging to recognize men as "victims" and still think of them as men. This socialization can make it less likely for men to seek services and can make it less likely that appropriate services are available.

Men who have been sexually victimized have a right to a full range of recovery services in settings that fully support their needs. Rape crisis centers should make every effort to ensure that volunteers and staff are trained on the needs and experiences of male victims; the availability of services for male victims is included in advertising and outreach; and the full range of services at the center, including support groups, is available to male victims.

MYTH: Males can't be sexually assaulted

REALITY: Men can be, and are, sexually assaulted every day. It can happen to any male, regardless of his sexual orientation, size, strength, appearance, occupation, race or culture. It happens at home, at work, in locker rooms and in cars — just about anywhere a perpetrator thinks he can get away with it. It's not unusual for a male victim to "freeze" out of shock or fear of physical harm. Few, if any, males have ever considered the possibility of such a thing happening, and are therefore totally unprepared.

MYTH: Only gay males are sexually assaulted

REALITY: The incidence of sexual assault involving gay male victims is slightly higher than for heterosexual males, but this is largely due to the fact that gay men can become the target of anti-gay violence perpetuated by other men. Heterosexual males can be, and are, sexually assaulted in large numbers.

MYTH: Only gay men sexually assault other males

REALITY: The vast majority of male offenders who sexually abuse or assault other men identify themselves as heterosexual. Some offenders target males simply because it gives them a greater feeling of dominance, power and control than abusing a woman. Sexual assault is usually much more about violence and anger than it is about lust or sexual attraction.

MYTH: Getting an erection or ejaculating during a sexual assault means the survivor "really wanted it" or even consented

REALITY: This myth causes major issues of guilt and confusion for all male survivors. Physical stimulation can cause an erection whether the recipient wants it to happen or not. Pressure in the prostate gland can cause the same reaction. Having an erection or ejaculation is a normal, involuntary physiological response, and does not automatically equate with arousal — or with consent. A male survivor may be bewildered or confused about his physiological response during the event, or may feel guilt or shame, and may therefore be inclined not to report it.

MYTH: Males who are sexually assaulted don't suffer as much as females who are assaulted: after all, they don't risk becoming pregnant

REALITY: All sexual assault survivors suffer many of the same reactions: depression, anger, anxiety, confusion, fear, numbness, self-blame, helplessness, suicidal feelings and shame are common ones. Some responses are gender specific, others are not. Sexual assault directed against gay men is more likely to involve higher levels of violence, use of weapons and multiple assailants. Statistically, male survivors are at higher risk of committing suicide. And while they don't become pregnant, male survivors of anal rape are at a high risk of internal damage, which leads to a greater possibility of HIV infection.

MYTH: Sexual assault between gay partners does not exist

REALITY: Sexual abuse and sexual assault can occur within any relationship. Through physical, psychological or emotional coercion, some gay men are forced by their partners to engage in non-consensual sexual acts. A gay man in a committed relationship is not the sexual property of his partner.

Source: Association of Alberta Sexual Assault Services. Website: www.aasas.ca

Healing After Sexual Assault

These are some of the symptoms Justin experienced. And the tools Justin used and will continue to use throughout his journey of healing.

Common sexual symptoms. The sexual effects that a survivor may experience after sexual abuse or sexual assault may be present immediately after the experience(s), or they may appear long afterwards. Sometimes the effects are not present until you are in a trusting and loving relationship, or when you truly feel safe with someone. The most common sexual symptoms after sexual abuse or sexual assault include:

1. Avoiding or being afraid of sex
2. Approaching sex as an obligation
3. Experiencing negative feelings such as anger, disgust, or guilt with touch
4. Having difficulty becoming aroused or feeling sensation
5. Feeling emotionally distant or not present during sex
6. Experiencing intrusive or disturbing sexual thoughts and images
7. Engaging in compulsive or inappropriate sexual behaviors
8. Experiencing difficulty establishing or maintaining an intimate relationship
9. Experiencing erectile or ejaculatory difficulties

Discovering your specific sexual symptoms is an important part of beginning sexual healing. It can be very upsetting to think about all the ways that the sexual assault or abuse has influenced you sexually, yet by knowing, you can begin to address those symptoms specifically. One way you can determine if you are about to engage in healthy sex is by asking yourself these questions.

CONSENT: Can I freely and comfortably choose whether or not to engage in sexual activity? Am I able to stop the activity at any time during the sexual contact?

EQUALITY: Is my feeling of personal power on an equal level with my partner? Does neither of us dominate the other?

RESPECT: Do I have a positive regard for myself and for my partner? Do I feel respected by my partner? Do I feel supportive of my partner and supported by my partner?

TRUST: Do I trust my partner on both a physical and emotional level? Do we have a mutual acceptance of vulnerability and an ability to respond to each other with sensitivity?

SAFETY: Do I feel secure and safe within the sexual setting? Am I comfortable with and assertive about where, when and how the sexual activity takes place? Do I feel safe from the possibility of STIs?

Automatic reactions to touch: Even after you have set up guidelines to make sexual activity feel safer, you may still experience automatic reactions to touch; such as a flashback, a panic attack, a sense of sadness, a sense of fear, dissociation, nausea, pain, or freezing.

These reactions are unwanted and upsetting to both you and your partner, though fortunately with time and healing they will minimize in frequency and severity.

In order to gain control of your body and mind during an automatic reaction, you want to ensure that you stop all sexual activity. Take time to make yourself aware of and acknowledge that you are having an automatic reaction. Try to consider what triggered it.

Once you have made yourself aware that you are experiencing an automatic reaction, take some time to calm yourself and make yourself feel safe again. Pay attention to your breathing, and try to take slow, deep breaths.

Take some time to bring your mind and body back to the present by reorienting yourself in your surroundings. Remind yourself that you are no longer living the sexual assault or abuse. Using your different senses, make yourself aware of your current environment. What do you see? What do you hear? Touch some of the objects around you to ground yourself to the present.

After you have overcome an automatic reaction, take some time to rest and recover. These reactions are overwhelming for both your body and mind. When you are ready, take some time to think about the trigger of your automatic reaction, and if there is some way you could alter the situation somehow so that the trigger does not happen or does not affect you in the same way. For example, perhaps changing the setup of the room would be helpful, or asking your partner not to do the activity that you believe may have set off your flashback.

Also, if you are being triggered while being intimate with a partner, discuss with your partner what you would like her/him to do when you have an automatic reaction (e.g. stop what they are doing, hold you, talk to you, sit with you, etc.) Ask your partner to watch for signs that you are having an automatic reaction, and to stop sexual activity immediately when you have one.

Sexual Healing Journey: If you are in a partnership at the time that you want to actively begin healing sexually, it is important that you work together. It is essential that you feel safe and comfortable with your partner and that your partner always respects your limits and is prepared to follow your lead throughout this process. Partners who act in ways that mimic sexual assault or abuse, such as touching without consent, ignoring how you feel, or behaving in impulsive or hurtful ways will prevent you from healing. Building emotional trust and a sense of safety in a relationship are important prerequisites to enjoying sexual intimacy again.

Resources:

University of Alberta Sexual Assault Centre

Incest and Sexuality: A Guide to Understanding and Healing by Wendy Maltz

The Survivor's Guide to Sex: How to Have an Empowered Sex Life After Child Sexual Abuse by: Staci Haines

The Courage to Heal: A Guide for Women Survivors of Child Sexual Abuse by Ellen Bass and Laura Davis

Victims No Longer: The Classic Guide for Men Recovering From Sexual Child Abuse by: Mike Lew

www.sexualhealth.com A website by the Sexual Health Network on sexuality and sexual recovery.

About the Author

Leigh Jarrett (she/he) is an unabashedly queer, quirky, and passionate author of Contemporary MM+ Romantic Fiction. Their published contemporary works include warm and always sexy HEA romances as well as dark romances filled with grit, trauma, and angst.

In their hometown of Victoria, BC, Canada, Leigh can be found nestled up with their fabulously supportive wife and trusty laptop or enjoying the wondrous Vancouver Island outdoors.

Please consider subscribing to Leigh's newsletter to stay up to date with their new releases and promos. If you're interested in MM+ Fantasy and Paranormal Romance, check out one of Leigh's other pen names, JT Fader, on their JT Fader Fantasticals website and newsletter jtfader.com.

To connect with Leigh Jarrett:

Email: leigh@leighjarrett.com

Website and newsletter: leighjarrett.com

You can also find Leigh on Bluesky

Other Books by Leigh Jarrett

"It all came down to a matter of trust."
A Friends to Lovers M/M Gay Romance
Snowblind

"Find love in the least expected place."
An Enemies to Lovers M/M Gay Romance

Merlot Rebellion

"Risking it all to follow your heart."
A Found Family M/M Bisexual Romance

Capital Adoration

"Brave enough to pursue love."
An Age Gap M/M Gay Romance

Pacific Pursuit

"Learning a new path to love."
A Roommates to Lovers Bisexual Awakening M/M Romance

Academic Adoration

"Recovering true love."
A Second Chance Hurt/Comfort M/M Romance

Drag Undivided

"Strumming your way to love."
A Grumpy/Sunshine Gay Awakening M/M Romance

Rhythmic Bliss